THE THING
ABOUT LOVE

THE THING ABOUT LOVE

LOUREVA SLADE

Productions

Published by MatildaBelle Productions

Los Angeles, CA

ISBN: 978-0997732900

Cover Design by Joshua Jadon
Back Cover Photo by Eboni Marmolejos

Table of Contents

Acknowledgments

Writing this collection of short stories has been a life-long dream. I must first thank God for giving me the creativity, desire, strength, and opportunity to actually do it. Thank you to my husband, Shannon, for all your support and encouragement and for reading and critiquing my stories. I thank my daughter, Amari Allen, for reading, editing, and providing feedback for every story in this collection. I truly appreciate you. To Michael Lugenbuehl, Wimberly Watson II, Sabrina Pierce, Akilah Crossland, and my writing mentor, Tamara Gregory, you all are amazing! Thank you, thank you, thank you for believing in me and pushing me to excellence. Thank you for all your help with editing and for pushing me toward my dream. To my baby girl, Halle Slade, thank you for allowing me to read my stories to you. It made me feel really special to know that you actually wanted to hear what mommy was writing.

To my mother and father, Wimberly and Bernice Watson, who both passed away in 2012, thank you for life and for the opportunities to do the things that I love. I love and miss you both so much. I am the woman I am today because of your patience and unconditional love.

Thanks for believing in me and telling me that I can do anything I want to do if I put my mind to it and work at it. I hope to honor your memories and always make you proud.

Behind Closed Doors

"The weak can never forgive. Forgiveness is an attribute of the strong."

-Mahatma Gandhi

"There is no love without forgiveness and there is no forgiveness without love."

-Bryant H. McGill

I sat undetected on the chocolate colored shag carpet in the dining room with my knees to my chest and my ear pressed against the golden oak French door with the faux gold knobs. Across the room, the midday sun beamed through the sliding glass doors that led to the patio and warmed the space around me. After years of wondering what the adults were discussing privately in the kitchen I eventually figured out that if I announced I had a lot of homework, turned the music on in my room, and tip-toed to the French doors that led into the kitchen, I could get my answers. With seven years under my belt, I had yet to be caught.

The fact that my sister, Angela, was the one talking privately with my mom was unfamiliar territory for me. But then again she was 24 years old, and I guess that did qualify her as an adult. But what was so important that she would miss work and make the six hour drive from San Jose to L.A. *alone* without having called ahead of time to say she was coming?

My sister and I had been so close before she went away to college. Even though I was ten years younger than Angela, she always treated me like I was her friend. I was like her shadow. We went everywhere together-the mall, the park, the movies. I looked up to her. I wanted to be perfect just like she was. I struggled to maintain a 3.833 GPA, with the goal of closing the semester with a 4.0 as she had done in the tenth grade. It seemed highly unlikely, but I tried nonetheless. I took piano lessons like she had. I was a part of all the extra-curricular activities that she had been a part of. I even planned to attend UCLA and join the same sorority that she had. I idolized her.

So naturally hearing Angela's sobs penetrating the door made me feel like someone was stabbing my heart with an icepick.

I could hear my mom hum and occasionally tell her that everything would be alright.

My heart ached.

I pictured my mother sitting next to my sister, holding her and rubbing her hair the way she did me when I had a bad day. I always found comfort in my mother's arms. I hoped Angela felt comforted as well.

"I feel so stupid," she finally said, her pitch an octave higher than usual.

My mother didn't respond. I imagined her searching for the right words to say.

"I want to forgive him, momma. I want us to work through this."

So this must be about her husband Alden, but that didn't make sense. I couldn't imagine him doing anything to purposely hurt my sister. They were college sweethearts and got married the weekend after they completed their Master's programs. Everyone always commented how perfect they were for each another- Alden, the Physician's Assistant and Angela, the I.T. guru.

I remember being extremely happy to hear that she was marrying someone like him. She had dated some total dweebs in high school-the illiterate college freshman who "just wanted to play pro ball," the quiet saxophonist with the hot temper who had been in anger management since elementary school, and the fine math scholar who was more feminine than Angela would ever be. So Alden, the intelligent, well-mannered, piano playing country boy was a breath of fresh air. He even sat at the piano with me for an hour the first time she introduced us to him and showed me how to play a gospel run. He was so patient with me and I was entranced by the way his fingers danced across the keys. I knew then he was a keeper. To think that perhaps Alden wasn't so perfect was inconceivable.

"Listen, honey, I've been where you are. I think I told you that my first husband cheated on me with my best friend. Talk about hurt. But truth is, he wasn't the one for me. If I hadn't been released from that marriage I never would have married your father."

"But I don't want to be with anyone else."

"I know, baby. That's my point. All things happen for a reason. You and Alden have something special-nothing like Otis and me. You and Alden are more like your father and I are. That man loves you. And you love him. People make mistakes, Angie. If you both want this marriage to work, trust me, you will get through this. God will heal your heart and this bump in the road will make your relationship stronger than ever. You just have to trust Him."

I couldn't believe what I was hearing. Alden cheated on Angela! No way should she consider staying with a man who would disrespect her in such a way. My mother was the one who told us not to tolerate infidelity under any circumstance. She told us that if a man cheats he obviously never loved you. If he cheats, it's over. Period.

I wanted to scream that into the kitchen. Scream some sense into my mother. Scream some sense into my sister.

Instead I sat silently and listened.

"I haven't told you the worst part."

Her voice cracked and her wailing began again.

I could hear my mother walk to the refrigerator and open the door. Once she closed it she turned on the faucet long enough to rinse off two Izze's, which were the only refreshments we kept around besides milk and water.

"What is it baby?" she finally asked after sitting down and cracking open the cans.

"He got her pregnant."

My heart dropped.

They didn't speak any words for what seemed like an eternity.

My mind raced. Cheating was one thing. Getting your mistress pregnant was a whole other issue. It warranted a walk to the gallows. No pardon granted. Permanent solitude for the cheater was a must. Why was Angela considering otherwise?

"Well. Do you want this marriage to work?"

"Nooooooo," my mind yelled and threw a temper tantrum in my brain.

"I do. More than anything," Angela answered quietly.

My heart sank.

"Do you know the other woman?" my mother asked.

"No. Alden said he met her at a card party that one of his co-workers threw a few months back. He said it was just a one-time thing-a mistake and he was sorry it had happened."

"A one-time thing?" My mother lost her cool for a second, which I could tell by the sarcastic way she asked the question. "What was Alden thinking? How could he be so reckless? There is too much at stake to be so-" her voice trailed off when Angela blew her nose.

My mother sighed loudly and said more calmly, "Last question for the day, Angie. Are you sure Alden wants it to work?"

"Mom, when he apologized, I know he meant it. He's been a wreck ever since it happened."

Silence. I could feel my heart beat as I tried to control my heavy breathing.

"He's a good man, momma. And I love him."

Their conversation had shaken my world more than a little bit. Love is many things but to hear that it could sometimes hurt was something I had never considered. To think of it pardoning the unpardonable attested to its strength.

"I'll be honest, sweetheart, it doesn't sound like the road ahead of you is going to be the easiest, but I do believe that beautiful endings can come from undesirable beginnings when God is involved. That's the thing about love. Whatever you do, don't beat yourself up for the decision you make. That is between you, your husband, and God. People are going to tell you that you should leave him. Some will say it because they love you and want you to be happy. Others because that's the textbook response to infidelity. But the truth is it doesn't matter what anyone else thinks. It doesn't matter what anyone else says they would do because no one really knows until, heaven forbid, they are faced with the same situation. Do you understand?"

"Yes."

"Now, Alden is going to need your love and support to get through this."

The rest of my mother's words ran together.

I stared at the red roses outside the sliding glass doors. They were positioned beautifully in front of the downtown sky line. The San Bernardino Mountains in the distance seemed so much closer than they actually were. I thought about how the roses in front of you will make you think that life is always filled with good times, but the truth is that it is really more like mountains-with ups and downs.

Did I believe Alden loved Angela? I was certain of it. I could tell by the way he looked at her. Did I believe he would ever cheat on Angela again? I honestly didn't get that feeling. Did I think I could ever forgive Alden for hurting my sister? If Angela was willing to forgive him, so was I.

I thought about my mother's counsel. Although she had given us the textbook response all our lives, when a real life situation arose, she gave advice that matched the love Angela and Alden felt for each other. It was advice that took into account that people make mistakes, God can fix what is broken, and that true love is worth giving a second chance. Looking at the beautiful scene outside I realized that throughout all the twists and turns, the ups and downs, the ebbs and flows, what is constant and what keeps you sane is your connection to Who is above. When that is right, you can overcome any obstacle you face-no matter how difficult it seems.

A chair slid across the linoleum. Ordinarily I would have rushed off to my room but today I sat motionless-trying to get my bearings straight after the rollercoaster on which my emotions had been. My sister opened the French doors and our eyes met. Her face was red and her eyes swollen. She opened her mouth but no words came out. I stared at her, my eyes like saucers. I wanted to hug her. Tell her I was sorry about what had happened. Tell her that she wasn't stupid. Tell her that I supported her. But I was unable to move. I was unable to speak. Angela looked like she had been through hell and back. She looked broken. Embarrassed. Weak. And for the first time in my life I saw her for exactly what she was-

Human.

And I loved her even more because of it.

The Thing about Love

"Love is patient, love is kind. It does not envy, it does not boast, it is not proud. It does not dishonor others, it is not self-seeking, it is not easily angered, it keeps no record of wrongs. Love does not delight in evil but rejoices with the truth. It always protects, always trusts, always hopes, always perseveres. Love never fails."

-1 Corinthians 13:4-8a

Friday night. Game night. The Washington Prep Generals had just put in serious work against the Manual Arts Toilers and shut it down 35-7. The air was still thick with excitement when the school bus packed with varsity players and cheerleaders approached the front of Washington Prep's football field. Terrence, the all-state quarterback who was sure to go pro, beat the seat in front of him and hollered out, "V-I-C-T-O-R-Y." All the students responded loudly, "VICTORY. VICTORY," as their red, white, and blue jerseys and uniforms swayed in unison to celebrate their final win of the regular season. No one thought it was possible for them to actually make it to the play-offs. Now that they had, their confidence was turned up a few notches.

While everyone else seemed to be caught up in the moment, Semaj's mind was focused on the future. He was entranced by the thought of actually playing college football. When the kids in elementary and middle school had talked about the colleges they would attend Semaj had always remained quiet or made comments about how you didn't have to go to college to be successful. The truth was that he wanted to go more than anything but knew early on that his mother was poor. No matter how many hours or jobs she worked, there was never enough. He couldn't dare ask a woman who already sacrificed so much to support him through college. Football opened up a world of opportunity for him. After all, he had skills. And because of those skills college was now a viable option.

Play-offs would begin in two weeks and Semaj had plans to really show off. The games would be packed with recruiters from all the greats-USC, UCLA, Notre Dame, Florida State, and Oregon. Semaj had been in talks with 'SC since his sophomore year. Now that he was a senior, he hoped to secure a spot on their team. He needed a full scholarship and had no intentions of being a walk-on. He had dreams of getting into sports management and knew that football was his free ticket to a first rate education.

"Hey Semaj. How late are you going to be up?" he heard a familiar voice in front of him ask.

Semaj looked up and realized that almost all the other players had already gotten off the bus. Chocolate Connie stood in front of him twirling her braids and popping gum. Her dark brown skin glistened in the bus's dim overhead lights. Her lips looked as if they had been freshly glossed and although she was the loudest and most spirited cheerleader on the squad, she smelled like sugar and spice and looked like everything nice.

Semaj flashed his thirty-two's at her.

"I'll be up late," he replied.

"Alright. I'mma holler at you," she said in her flirty voice. "Oh, and you held it down tonight."

"Thanks," Semaj blushed.

The walk home from games was usually a quick one, but tonight something was different. Semaj headed down Denker and cut right on 113th Street. Every so often someone from the team would ride by, honk, and holler, "V-I-C-T-O-R-Y." Each time Semaj nodded his

head, threw up a peace sign, and yelled, "VICTORY."
This felt good. Victory really was sweet and he was a few
steps closer to the success for which he longed.

As Semaj approached the steps to the front door of
their Spanish-style home, he could see his mother sitting
on the porch waiting anxiously for details about the
game. He put on his most realistic sad face and hung his
head.

"Hey baby. How'd it go?" she asked gently.

"Not too good, momma."

"Oh baby," she said and held out her arms.

"Not too good for the other team. Momma, we won!
We're going all the way," Semaj said as he hugged his
mother and lifted her off her feet.

"What?" his mother screamed excitedly. "Semaj
Johnson, I'm gonna beat your butt, boy. Don't do that
to me! You know my heart can't take it," she said
laughing as he set her back on her feet.

"I was just messing with you," he laughed.

"How many touchdowns did my star running back
make?" she asked.

"Two."

"That's my boy! Play-off time! I hope I can get the time off to come see you play."

Semaj hoped so too.

His mother smiled and then sighed. "You remind me so much of your father."

He didn't know how to respond. He hated being compared to his father, but his mother constantly did it. And Semaj could tell by the tone of his mother's voice that she missed him more than ever on nights like these.

He sucked his teeth and stared blankly at her to show that he was uncomfortable with the turn the conversation was taking.

"Speaking of your father," she continued, ignoring his discomfort, "He sent you another letter. It's on your desk. I'm pretty sure he would love it if you actually wrote him back this time."

"Here we go again," Semaj said. He hadn't wanted to be disrespectful, but he really didn't feel like talking about his father-especially not after such a great game. His mother knew how Semaj felt about James and yet she made it a point to tell him three things he didn't really want to hear within a matter of seconds-Semaj was just like his father, his father had written yet another letter, and Semaj should write him back. The latter wasn't happening.

"I'm not going there with you Semaj. I just know that I've raised you better than to treat anyone the way you've treated him. Whether you like it or not he's your father and he needs you right now."

"I've needed him my whole life," he said angrily as he thought about all the important things James had missed-school plays, award ceremonies, talent shows, camping trips, every single football game, and ten years of Semaj's growing pains. He had needed his father, but his father had *chosen* not to be there. And Semaj refused to excuse his absence.

She didn't respond.

Semaj pushed through the barred front door, went into his bedroom, threw his bags on the bed, and slammed the door behind him. Shortly afterward he heard his mother close the front door and walk to her room.

It didn't matter how many people told him how talented his father was, or how athletic he was, or anything else, Semaj could never forgive him.

Semaj's name was James spelled backwards, and Semaj was determined to be the exact opposite of his father. He would never get involved in gangs. He would never abandon his wife and child. He would never hang out with murderers. Instead he would go to college, earn good money, and take care of his responsibilities. He was on the path to do just that.

Semaj picked up his father's latest pencil written letter. James had drawn a picture of a samurai warrior on the back. His father really could have been an artist, but he had thrown it all away for an undeserving murderer.

Semaj opened the letter and read:

October 23, 2014

Son,

This guy on my block gave his life to Christ today. It's been a long time in the making. He's been in for three years-convicted on drug charges. Every time I got a moment to holler at him on the yard I told him about Jesus. A few months ago he started attending the bible study they have here and then today he finally made the decision to live for Christ. I'm glad he made that choice.

I don't recommend jail to anyone, but I will say that I can see the Lord moving in here in a real way. I'm so much different now than I was when I got here because of my personal relationship with Him. I've witnessed so many other men change too-God is alive and real, son. Don't forget that.

If I timed this letter correctly, you had a big game today. I already know how you did-you're MY son. I was the man back when I was your age.

I'm proud of you. Your mom says you're planning to go to college and you're making good grades. I'm glad you never got mixed up with foolishness like I did. Life would be real different had I made the smart choices you're making.

I just want you to know that I love you. I wish you would write me back, but I know how it is. I was 17 once too.

Tell your mom I love her.

Dad

A tear trickled down Semaj's face. He hated that as much as he disliked his father, he hadn't been able to stop loving him. And he missed him. But he wanted him to hurt the same way he did, and although he always read

James' letters, he refused to write him back. Writing back would imply that everything was ok, but it wasn't.

Semaj thought about the good times they shared as if they happened just yesterday. He went everywhere with his father. Although some of the places weren't kid-appropriate, Semaj had been his father's road dog. James had taught him how to play football when Semaj was five. They would go outside, toss the ball, and tackle one another. Life was sweet until the day James was arrested for murder. Semaj would never forget the day his father was put into the back of that police car. He had looked so weak-so defeated. It was the last time Semaj had seen him. He was seven years old at the time.

Semaj had heard that his father hadn't actually committed the murder, but was serving time because he wouldn't snitch on the person who really pulled the trigger. Thinking that his father forfeited raising him to protect a random thug really bothered Semaj. How could he give up his son to protect a hoodlum? There wasn't an acceptable answer-and that hurt.

His father talked about Jesus in every letter, but Semaj didn't want to hear it. It seemed to him prisoners were so bored that they all had spiritual awakenings on the inside. Whether they converted to Islam, Buddhism, Christianity, or whatever, they always converted to *something*. He knew they would quickly drop the Jesus talk if ever they got paroled. His father's words sounded sincere, but he wouldn't be surprised if it was all a front.

Semaj balled up the letter and threw it away.

He turned on the radio and headed to the shower to wash away the evening's excitement.

When he got back to his room, he saw three missed calls from Chocolate Connie. He moved his bags off his bed and returned her call. She sounded like she was still chewing bubble gum.

"Hey Semaj," she said.

"Hey, Chocolate. What are you doing?"

"Thinking about you," she said.

Semaj smiled. Chocolate Connie wasn't the type of girl who talked to high school guys, but she talked to him. She said it was because he was more mature than the other guys at school.

"You were looking good tonight," he said in his smooth, trying to sound sexy, voice.

"You got me over here cheesing," she replied. She sounded like she was twirling her braids when she said it.

"What are you getting into tomorrow?" Semaj asked.

"Chillin."

"Meet me at the Del Amo mall," he said.

"Fa sho. What time?"

"Twelve o'clock," he answered.

"Ok. I'll text you in the morning to let you know if I can go. You know how my mom is," Connie said.

"It's all good. I'm 'bout to go eat dinner and then go to sleep. I'm super tired, but I'll get at you tomorrow," Semaj said.

"Goodnight, sexy," she said.

Semaj hung up the phone and thought how he and Chocolate Connie never actually did any of the things they planned. He knew that her mother didn't care for him because of his family's economic status. She was one of those bourgeois types. The phone conversations and hanging out at school were good enough for him. One day he would prove to be "the man."

Semaj went into the kitchen and saw that his mother had put a plate of his favorites-pot roast, mashed potatoes and green beans in the refrigerator for him. He pulled it out and warmed it in the microwave.

A few minutes after he sat down, his mother came into the kitchen and sat in the chair across from him.

"This food is good, ma," he complimented.

"Thank you, sweetheart. I figured you would need some victory food," she said.

He smiled.

"Look, there's something I need to talk to you about and I need you to hear me all the way out," she said.

"What's up?" he asked.

"I just got off the phone with your dad's old friend, Darren, and he told me that the guy your dad is serving time for was murdered earlier today."

Semaj rolled his eyes and wondered where this was leading. He was so tired of hearing about his father, the murder, and the man who actually committed the crime. He didn't want to know nor did he care about the details.

"Don't you know what this means?" his mother asked excitedly.

"That he got what he deserved?" he asked and took a bite of his potatoes.

"No. It means that your father can tell the truth without worrying about retaliation. I'm certain they'll release him early once they know the truth."

Semaj remained silent.

"So I need a favor," his mother continued.

Semaj looked at her without speaking and took a bite of roast.

"I need you to come with me to the jail in the morning to tell your father the news," she said.

Semaj took a sip of red Kool-aid to wash down the roast that was now stuck in his throat.

"You want me to do what?" he asked incredulously once he had cleared his throat.

"Now look, I don't ever ask you for much of anything, but I really want you to come with me tomorrow when I deliver the news to your father. And I'm sure he would love to see you. It's been too long."

"That's not my fault, ma. He made that choice," Semaj said angrily.

"Look. I understand your frustration, but your father is a really good man. That's why I love him. How do you think I feel? It hurts that my husband is in prison. It hurts even more to know that he hasn't been here to see you grow up-especially when I've seen how much it hurts you. But your father is loyal to a fault. I don't agree with the decision he made ten years ago either, but I can see now that God had a plan. And honestly, he's a much better man now than he was then. He probably would have been dead had he been on the outside. I thank God that I can still hold him, touch him, and see his face."

"I'm glad you feel that way, but I don't."

Neither said a word for a few minutes. Then his mother broke the silence.

"I'm leaving tomorrow morning at 6:30 and I want you to go with me. You don't have to go in to see him, but I want you to at least ride and support me. You owe me that much," she said firmly.

Semaj grit his teeth. His appetite had completely left him.

"May I be excused?" he asked.

His mother nodded.

He threw the majority of his food in the trash, swallowed his last sip of Kool-aid, rinsed his dishes off, and placed them in the sink.

He walked to his bedroom, closed the door, and plopped on his bed. Hot angry tears streamed from the corners of his eyes and left puddles on his pillows.

Ironically, Tupac's "I Ain't Mad at Cha" came on the radio at the exact moment Semaj was thinking about how upset he was with his father. Although the song was about the friendship between 'Pac and his buddy, the chorus resounded in Semaj's mind. Part of him wished he could say that to his father, but it wasn't true. He *was* mad at him. He picked up his remote and switched off the radio. His room would have been completely dark had it not been for the moon's illumination and the faint light from his alarm clock. Semaj took a few deep breaths.

He didn't want to escort his mother to the prison.

It was true that his mother never asked him to do much of anything, aside from the normal things sons were asked to do-take out the trash, keep his room clean, and mow the lawn. And she was extremely understanding when he fell short of finishing his chores because of practice or school projects.

He would *have* to go with her tomorrow morning. But he wouldn't do it cheerfully. He resolved to sleep during the car ride and say as few words as possible.

He looked at the clock on his nightstand. It was 12:06am-too late to text Chocolate Connie and cancel their date. He would do it first thing in the morning.

Semaj stared at the USC banner and the posters of his heroes taped on the wall opposite his bed. The eyes of Pete Carroll, Cam Newton, Bobby Wagner, and Reggie Bush seemed to stare back at him-reminding him that making it through each days' obstacles would place him one step closer to achieving his goals.

Semaj looked out his window at the brick wall that was just steps from it. He heard a helicopter overhead. Its sound was such a normal part of life that he couldn't imagine a week going by without hearing it. But as he lay there, he hoped for the day he would be successful enough to provide his mother with the life his father had been unable to provide. He hoped to give her the life she deserved-one where she would never hear choppers in the midnight skies.

When Semaj and his mother stepped into the visiting area, he felt extremely tense. That morning his mother had made him a nice breakfast and told him that she hoped he would go in with her. She said it would make her happy if he would be with her when she delivered the good news. She threw in another round of punches, reminding him that she never asked him for anything and had worked hard to provide for him. It didn't take a whole lot of effort for her to guilt him into it.

His mother had borrowed her best friend's car, as she did every Saturday she went to visit James. Although it was a thirty year-old Cutlass, it was reliable. It always got her safely to the prison. Semaj and his mother didn't do much talking during the two and a half hour car ride to Delano. His mother set the radio dial to National Public Radio and he stared out the window when he wasn't feigning sleep. Semaj enjoyed the details of their news stories. He felt like he could hold an intelligent conversation about things that normally didn't interest him after listening to just an hour of their programming. The skies outside were gray, but the weatherman had just reported that temperatures would make it up to the low seventies by mid-day. Semaj hoped their trip would be quick so he could get back in time to play a little flag football with his neighborhood crew.

Semaj couldn't stop thinking about how uncomfortable this whole trip made him. Even the thought of his father possibly coming home sooner than later made him uneasy. For ten years Semaj had been the only man in his household. He had no idea what it would be like for his father to assume his rightful position. And although his father seemed to be on a righteous path, he wondered whether he would remain a changed man once he was back on his old block.

When they arrived, Semaj felt a tinge of guilt because the trip hadn't taken nearly as long as he imagined it would. In ten years he hadn't been to see his father a single time. When he was younger, his mother kept him away to "protect" him. She had said it was because his dad ran with the wrong crowd and she didn't want Semaj tied up in any foolishness. She even spoke venomously about him for a couple months, but then all of a sudden she changed. She started accepting his phone calls and visited him on weekends. By the time she felt Semaj was old enough to visit his father, Semaj's desire for a relationship with James had dissipated-and so had his respect for him. Now he was ashamed of himself.

When they walked into the visiting area, Semaj was shocked to see so many people. It was only 9:30 am, but there were at least a hundred people already seated with their loved ones. There was a small television on one side of the room, where young children sat watching a cartoon. Vending machines lined the walls and a few officers were positioned around the room in case things got out of hand. Inmates dressed in light blue shirts and dark blue pants sat at tables with their visitors, and although Semaj had never met any of them, their faces showed pure appreciation for the ones who had taken the time to visit.

Semaj continued to scan the room before his eyes fell upon a lone prisoner sitting at a table. When their eyes met, his father stood and a broad smile spread across his face. Semaj's mother walked toward her husband, but Semaj stood frozen, not sure of how he felt. His mother looked back and beckoned him to come. With each step he took, his anger and resentment seemed to dissolve.

Everyone had told him how much he looked like his father, and seeing him in person, Semaj couldn't deny their resemblance. His father looked a lot different than his pictures from younger years. In his pictures, he had looked menacing, but in person, there was no trace of the criminal he had imagined his father to be. Perhaps his mother was right. Maybe prison had actually been good for him.

Semaj watched as his mother embraced his father. He could tell that she was beyond thrilled to see him and he felt slightly jealous about sharing her affection. His father closed his eyes and gave her a kiss on the cheek. After their embrace, she stepped to the side and said, "They won again last night," and looked at Semaj.

James looked at his son. Semaj could see pride oozing out of him.

"Son," he said and extended his arms for an embrace.

When Semaj had imagined this moment earlier, he saw himself sitting off to the side and not saying a word to his father, but now that he was face to face with the man who had given him life he couldn't help but fall into his father's massive arms. All he felt was love. It overpowered every other feeling he had ever felt.

He remembered beat boxing with his father. He remembered watching television with his father. He remembered his father taking him to the park. He remembered his father's infectious laugh. He remembered his father's encouraging words. He remembered all the love that he had chosen to forget. He was ashamed of the way he had treated a man who had loved him so much.

He thought about all the letters his father had written. He thought about the many trips his mother had taken to see him-trips that he refused to take with her. He thought about how much time had passed and how much of his life his father had missed-in part because of James's choices, but in larger part because of Semaj's choice to stay away.

As they hugged, Semaj wept. If his teammates saw him now, they would be surprised to see the 6'3" 200 pound receiver bawling like a baby over his father, a man he rarely mentioned.

"I'm so glad to see you, son" James said, tears streaming down his face as well. "This is an answer to my prayers."

The lump in Semaj's throat made it difficult to speak, but even if he had been able to speak, he didn't quite know what to say.

His mother took a seat, and the two men followed suit. Semaj dried his face with his shirt sleeve and looked up to see his father doing the same.

"How have you been?" James asked, looking at Semaj. His voice sounded like the Allstate guy's.

"I've been alright," Semaj said. From the corner of his eye he could see his mother smiling as she, too, wiped tears from her eyes.

"I haven't heard from you in a long time," James said. "Do you read the letters I send?"

"I read 'em," Semaj answered ashamedly and shifted in his seat.

"I understand. I was your age once. I know how hard this has been on you and I just want you to know that I am sorry. If I could do things all over again, a lot would be different."

Semaj fidgeted with his sweaty hands before folding them on the table. If he could do things all over again, he would do some things differently too.

"I know you may not believe it, son, but I love you. And I'm proud of you."

Semaj nodded his head. He wanted to tell his dad that he loved him too, but he couldn't make the words come out of his mouth. It was like a part of him wanted to remain bitter even though the larger part longed to let go of all the hurt and pain.

"James," his mother said, breaking the awkward silence, "I have some great news. Well actually, let me just say I have some news."

"What's up, sweetheart?" his father asked.

It was strange to hear his mother and father talk after so many years. He knew she visited him often and that they talked regularly on the phone, but to actually see them interact felt strange. His mother was so comfortable, and his father's tone, very loving. He could tell they were best friends.

"I'm not sure if you heard, but Anthony was murdered yesterday. Darren called and told me last night."

James seemed shocked-shaken up.

Semaj's mother put her hand on James's hand and he shed a few more tears. These were tears of sorrow.

Semaj looked down at his own hands. It truly hurt to see his father in pain.

"I'm sorry to hear that," James said. "I wrote him letters about the Lord all the time, but he never responded to my pleas for him to give his life to Christ. I sure hope he accepted Him before he died. The alternative is-," his voice trailed off.

Semaj looked up and saw the sincerity in his father's eyes.

"How is his family?" James asked.

"Darren didn't mention them, he just told me about Anthony."

James sat silent for a few moments. Semaj's mother continued to rub his hand.

"Do you think that you can tell the authorities that he was the one who committed the murder all those years ago? That will help you get out of here sooner."

James didn't respond.

"If you want me to talk with your attorney, say the word. I will call him as soon as we leave here."

James looked as if he didn't know how to process all that his wife was saying, but he finally spoke, "I just can't believe that I might be able to see Semaj walk across the stage. I've been praying for that since the day I was sentenced."

"I know," his mom said. "Won't God make a way?"

"Please contact my attorney. I'm ready to get out of here. I'm ready to be your full-time husband. Semaj, I'm ready to be your full-time dad," he said with a sincere smile.

Semaj looked at his father for a moment before darting his eyes back to his hands.

"Do you hear that, son? Your old man has a lot of time to make up for," James said.

"Yes sir," Semaj answered, surprised by the respect he felt for the man who sat before him.

With tears in his eyes, James asked, "Have you ever made a wrong choice while playing football?"

Semaj nodded his head.

"In life, sometimes we make wrong choices. And sometimes one wrong choice can have awful consequences. But that choice doesn't define you. I made lots of bad choices. I put my loyalties in the wrong places, but it was all a part of God's plan."

Semaj looked into his father's earnest eyes. He did understand.

The room started to feel smaller. The overhead fluorescent lights flickered. Despite the busyness all around, Semaj was keenly focused on his thoughts and the hum of the vending machines.

The last two days had been emotional. From winning the game, to seeing his father for the first time in ten years-from feeling near-hatred for his father, to feeling excitement about the possibility of having him home. Semaj could feel his temperature rising-the way it did in the hours preceding a big game. He needed to collect his thoughts and cool off.

Semaj looked at his mother and asked politely, "May I go wait in the car?"

His mother looked at James and then back at her son.

"Go ahead, Semaj," James answered. "And thanks for coming out, man. I've been missing you so bad. It's good to see that your mom has done such a great job with you. We talk about you all the time, but to actually have you here and to hear your voice, man! You have no idea how that makes me feel. It's an answered prayer. I love you, son."

Semaj looked into his father's eyes and from the very depths of his being came the four words he hadn't imagined himself ever saying to James again, but especially not today.

"I love you, too."

After he uttered the words, it was as if time stopped- or rather as if it finally started again.

Both James and Semaj stood up, shook hands, and pulled in for a warm embrace.

Semaj looked at him a few more moments before he headed to the door that led into the lobby. He could feel his father's eyes watching as he exited.

Semaj had heard that love is the strongest force in the universe. He had heard that it was stronger than hurt, pain, and anger. Now, he was certain that all he had heard was true. He still hadn't fully grasped the concept of having a strong relationship with his father, but he no longer denied that it was possible. When Semaj reached the door, he looked back. His eyes met his father's. Semaj smiled, nodded, and walked out.

Saturday afternoon. Game day. The USC Trojans had just put in serious work against the UCLA Bruins and shut it down 35-7. The air was still thick with excitement. Before exiting the field, Semaj looked in the stands. His mother hollered out enthusiastically and waved. Semaj smiled and waved back. He caught his father's tear-filled eyes. Semaj pumped his fist in the air. His father smiled and did the same.

James had proven to be the reformed man of his letters. After seeing the changes God had made in his father's life, Semaj was happy to give his life to Christ and experience the same peace and assurance his father had known even in the confined space of a prison cell.

Semaj was thankful for all that God had done for his family. He had protected them. He had saved them. He had restored his relationship with James. The past ten years hadn't been perfect, but his parents had been right. God had a plan. And he was thankful that God's plan included an opportunity for him to know both his father and his Father.

The Un-Jilting of Rachel

"The greatest sense of love, which is available for us at all times, is God's love."

- Stormie Omartian,

Choose Love Book of Prayers

Rachel sat on a red and white square blanket under a large broad-leaf tree in Cheviot Hills Park. With her thin legs folded beneath her, Rachel scrolled through the text messages on her iPhone for the hundredth time to make sure she hadn't gotten the time or date wrong. The text from Mike said to meet him here at 12 o'clock today. It was a quarter past one. She had already called and texted him a few times but he hadn't responded.

She clicked onto his BeSocial page. As few as two minutes ago, he had liked a picture of a Tesla and commented, "Wish I was driving this right now." Rachel couldn't believe her eyes. He was commenting on pictures of cars when he was supposed to be with her. She clicked under his comment and typed, "@mike_squarepants I can't stand liars…especially not at 1:15."

She clicked onto her own profile and updated her status. "Disappointed. Again."

Rachel set her phone down and took a deep breath.

Why was it so difficult for her to find love? And why did guys think it was ok to talk with her on the phone, plan picnics in the park, and then just stand her up? Why did it seem impossible to find a single man she could trust to be completely honest with her-someone who would actually show up? Rachel knew one thing-she was never going to talk to Mike again. Even if he texted her and apologized and even if he sent her a dozen roses there was no way she would excuse the pain and embarrassment she felt in this moment.

A bluebird landed on a picnic table not too far from where Rachel sat. She noticed how small and delicate the little bird was. She couldn't help but feel a little envious of the bird because it wouldn't ever have to deal with a broken heart.

Matthew 6:26 immediately came to her mind.

"Look at the birds of the air; they do not sow or reap or store away in barns, and yet your heavenly Father feeds them. Are you not more valuable than they?"

Am I not more valuable than that bird, Lord?

Rachel wondered.

She hoped to hear an audible response from her invisible God, but He said nothing.

Rachel wiped a tear from her eye and decided to try and make the best of her day. She wanted to have a really *good* cry-the kind that would take a couple days to recover from. But she would have to wait until she got home for that. Rachel dug into a brown picnic basket that she had neatly packed for her first meeting with Mike and pulled out a ham sandwich. She took a bite but found it difficult to get the food past the familiar lump in her throat. She put the sandwich back in the bag and the bag back in the basket.

Just as Rachel contemplated heading home, an elderly couple she had noticed when she first arrived made eye contact with her, smiled, and headed in her direction.

Oh great, she thought and tensed up. She wasn't in the mood for small talk.

As they approached her, the old lady smiled brightly and said, "Young lady, I just had to come and tell you how nice you look. I really like that bow in your hair."

"Really?" Rachel asked, sensing the lady's genuineness. She relaxed. *How sweet,* she thought. "Thank you," she said and blushed.

"I had one just like it when I was your age. I guess it's true that all styles come back, huh?" the old lady asked and glanced at her husband. He smiled and nodded.

"I guess so," Rachel said, returning her smile.

"Are you meeting someone?" the old lady asked.

"I was supposed to. But he never showed up."

"His loss," the old lady said with a knowing smile.

"Thank you," Rachel said, wishing she believed the old lady.

"Trust me. God has better for you. He's working everything out for your good."

Jeremiah 29:11 and Romans 8:28, Rachel thought.

"I hope so."

The old man nudged the old lady and she looked at her watch before hurriedly saying, "Well it was so nice to talk with you, young lady. And don't forget to smile. It's a beautiful day and God loves you."

Rachel smiled politely and nodded as the couple headed toward the parking lot.

Rachel sighed. That brief exchange had actually made her feel a little better.

Rachel exhaled and noticed that the temperature had seemed to drop a few degrees since she first arrived. She was no longer sweating as she had been an hour ago. It felt like it was probably about 75 degrees-the perfect temperature.

From the corner of her eye she spotted something small and furry scurrying toward a nearby ficus tree. She turned to see an adorable squirrel. He seemed to notice her at the same time she turned and he stopped just long enough to smile at her. (At least it looked like a smile.)

The squirrel's eyes were black pearls. His bushy tail wagged excitely as he continued on to climb the tree's pale brown trunk. He stopped abruptly after jumping onto one of its low branches. The squirrel looked out at the park grounds below and seeming pleased, laid down on the branch and closed his eyes.

The leaves rustled as the wind blew ever so gently. Rachel noticed that the tree's outstretched branches and leaves formed a perfect circle. As her eyes continued upward, beyond the tree, she was awed by the brilliant color of sky. It was the most enchanted blue she had ever seen, with white cumulous clouds sprinkled throughout.

It was a beautiful day, indeed.

With her eyes fixed above, Rachel felt an overwhelming sensation that she had often felt and ignored in the past. She felt a prodigious sense of peace. It was as if her disappointment just dissipated. The breeze blew the leaves around her and Rachel smiled.

It finally made sense.

The change in plans, the bluebird, the "silence," the old lady, the perfect weather, the adorable squirrel, the gentle breeze, the fluffy clouds, and the lovely sky. They had all been strategically placed to draw her attention back to Him-the Lover of Her Soul. The feeling that she had felt so often before but ignored was the feeling of *true love* from her Heavenly Father.

What had seemed like silence had been Him speaking all along.

Another tear rolled down Rachel's cheek. This time it was a tear of joy.

Rachel thought about being jilted by Mike and thanked God for protecting her from what she couldn't see. Her heart was extremely fragile, and God, in his omniscience, knew that the two of them wouldn't be a good fit. He obviously did have better for her, as the old lady had suggested, and Rachel could finally see it.

Rachel thought about how often random strangers would spot her out and talk to her about God. It wasn't as if they were trying to convert her. It was more like they knew she was a believer and just had something to get off their chests. And it was interesting that the scriptures or words these random strangers spoke often ministered to exactly what *she* herself was going through at that moment. She realized now that God had been speaking to her through people all along.

God loved her. He *absolutely* loved her. She was intensely aware of it now.

In church a few weeks ago, a guest speaker had said that God wants to be our everything. He desires an intimate and personal relationship with us. The speaker had said that God wants us to have His absolute best, but we must seek Him first.

All that had sounded good at the time, but the problem was that she couldn't actually see God. Rachel wanted something tangible. She wanted to feel love's touch. She wanted to be held in someone's arms and made to feel special. But now that she was paying attention, she could see that He had been there all along-loving her deeply.

Rachel felt God's undivided attention directly upon her. Her body tingled at the thought. There was no one or nothing in this world that could make her feel as ecstatic as she did in this moment. After closing her eyes and thanking Him for His love, she invited Him to have a seat and dine with her.

And there, in Cheviot Hills Park, where birds chirped, children played, and cars whizzed by on Pico and Motor, Rachel shared a meal with God and she basked in His love-*true* LOVE.

The First Lady's Daughter

"Above all, love each other deeply, because love covers over a multitude of sins."

- 1Peter 4:8

Things were good, thank God. After years as the subject of much gossip, Debra had finally gained the respect she deserved as the first lady of True Discipleship Church. She sat smugly in her usual position on the second pew from the pulpit and smiled as she hummed along with the soloist who sang, "I Won't Complain." The Deaconess and Mother's Board ladies positioned around her wore white dresses, white gloves, and white knit hats. She was the youngest of the group, but she was happy to fit in.

Debra caught a glance from her husband and winked at him. He smiled and returned the wink. He'd be at the podium soon-his powerful voice commanding the small congregation-and she wanted him to know that she supported him.

Her husband was truly a man of God, and he had loved her enough to see beyond her many shortcomings and make an honest woman out of her. Sure she had to sacrifice a lot to be the wife of such a prominent man, but he had sacrificed too. And he was worth it.

She closed her eyes for a moment and swayed from side to side. She listened as Sis. Virginia sang like a woman with a testimony. Seconds later she felt a hand on her arm. She opened her eyes and a plump usher stooped next to her and whispered, "Sis. Porter, your *daughter* is in the vestibule and wants to talk to you. She said it's *very* important."

Debra's eyes widened as she bit her bottom lip nervously. *Which daughter?*

"Thank you, Sis. Logan," she said and nodded.

Debra stood up, lowered her head, lifted her gloved right index finger, and quickly made her way to the swinging wood doors at the rear of the sanctuary.

The smell of marijuana accosted Debra's nostrils even before she made it into the vestibule, and she immediately knew which daughter so urgently needed to talk with her. She took a deep breath and hoped for the best.

Debra gasped at the sight of Lucinda. Her oldest daughter had once been such a beautiful girl-beautiful enough to model, in fact. But modeling and gangbanging didn't coincide. And of the two, Lucinda preferred the power afforded by the latter. Debra speechlessly examined her daughter's bruised and swollen face. Lucinda's pregnant belly was obvious despite the baggy clothes she wore.

Debra looked around to make sure no one was watching. She caught the glimpse of an usher peering through the partly open swinging door. He quickly turned away when Debra spotted him.

"Who did this to you?"

"I'm alright, momma," Lucinda's eyes avoided Debra's.

"Who did this to you, Lucinda?" Debra demanded.

"Let's just say that I handled it."

"Handled it?"

"Yeah. Only she got it worse," Lucinda said, seeming remorseful.

"How far along are you?"

"Seven months. It's a girl."

"The father?"

"He's dead to me."

"I'm sorry to hear that."

"You and me both, but shit happens."

"Why didn't you call to tell me you're pregnant?"

"You told me *not* to call. Just trying to respect your household," Lucinda said, still avoiding her mother's eyes.

"Well congratulations. Children are always a blessing," Debra said, feeling the irony. She never imagined finding out about her first grandchild this way, but she'd never imagined most of the things life had thrown her way.

So much time had passed and so much had happened in the two years since she'd seen her oldest daughter. She wished that things hadn't gone down the way they had. But as long as Lucinda was living the gang life it was best to love her from a distance. A thug daughter didn't fit the mold that she and the reverend had created for themselves. And anything that didn't fit had been cut loose. Period.

Debra turned and saw two nosy ushers looking through a crack in the door. They didn't turn away and she could hear them whispering. She knew the gossip was going to start back up soon and she loathed the thought of it all, but since the reverend had made it clear that her daughter wasn't welcome in their home, she had to talk here if she was going to talk at all.

"You smell like you've been smoking. That can't be good for the baby," Debra said as she placed a gentle hand on her daughter's belly.

"Look, I've been stressed the hell out. I didn't come here for you to judge me," Lucinda said and took a step back.

"I'm not judging you, sweetheart."

"I just wanted to tell you that I'm in some pretty deep shit. I've gotta get out of Killa Cali for a little while. Lay low."

What kind of stuff?

"Where are you going?" Debra asked.

"To stay with some homies in Arizona."

Debra shook her head, worried. *Who were these homies? Who had beaten her like that and why?* Questions layered upon questions and her heart ached for her daughter. It hurt to think of her dealing with all this on her own.

Seeming to recognize her mother's anguish, Lucinda added, "Don't trip. I'mma be alright."

Debra's eyes fixed on the cross pendant that hung from a gold chain on Lucinda's neck.

"The blood of Jesus covers a multitude of sins," Debra murmured.

"That's what you always told me. I've sinned more than a little bit and I'm tired of it. I sure hope the whole forgiveness thing is true. 'Cause I really want to change. I just can't seem to do that here."

Debra looked at her daughter and recognized her sincerity. She was proud of Lucinda, indeed.

"I love you, baby girl," Debra whispered. "I'm so sorry I-"

"No need to apologize. You did what you thought was best. I get it...and I love you too."

Debra hugged her daughter tighter than she had in a long time.

"Tell my sisters I love them. And tell your husband I said what's up. I'll call you once I touch down. And please pray for me," Lucinda pleaded.

Debra nodded. "Always."

Just as soon as Lucinda walked out the church doors Debra heard female voices yell, "What up, blood? Six Deuce Brims!" After a flood of profanities filled the air, Debra honed in on her daughter's cries as shots rang out.

Debra froze momentarily before hitting the floor, as she had done so many times during her own youth.

She heard tires screech and her heart ached because it knew what her eyes had not yet seen.

Debra pushed through the door leading to the street. Lucinda's lifeless body lay on the concrete. Blood oozed out of her head. Her neck. Her stomach. Debra rushed to her daughter's side and held her in her arms, blood staining her white gloves and dress as her tears flowed uncontrollably. She no longer cared who saw her and was ashamed that she hadn't stopped caring long before this moment. Her daughter-a piece of herself-was dead. She screamed for all of Heaven and earth to hear.

"My baby! Oh God! Somebody call 9-1-1!"

Lori's Assignment

(Inspired by the story of Jonah)

"'Love the Lord your God with all your heart and with all your soul and with all your mind and with all your strength.' The second is this: 'Love your neighbor as yourself.' There is no commandment greater than these."

-Mark 12:30-31

"Obedience is better than sacrifice."

-1 Samuel 15:22

He'd asked her to do some difficult things in the past-start a prison ministry, provide a couple transitional work opportunities for homeless young adults, and even travel to Hong Kong to minister to college students about salvation. Despite the logistical challenges, once Lori received her assignments, she worked diligently to do all that was asked of her. It was an honor to be about her Father's business.

His most recent request, however, was something she just flat-out did not want to do.

"Go," He had said, "And tell her of My love."

Lori, not at all wanting to believe that God would ask her to talk to such a loathsome woman about His love hadn't responded well. "Why?" she'd asked indignantly.

"I have a plan for her," He responded. "She belongs to me. I need her to know that I love her."

"I can't," Lori had said without hesitation. "There has to be some other way."

"Go," He repeated, "And tell her of My love."

The conversation was over.

That was exactly two weeks ago. Although Lori still sat on her patio and sipped hot tea each morning, and although she still read scriptures from her bible and kept a journal and pen nearby to record revelations from her prayer time, she hadn't heard anything at all since His request of her two weeks ago. She'd hoped He would just give her a different assignment, but she hadn't been so lucky.

At 7:15am, as usual, Lori could hear the bass line of a detestable rap song pumping through the walls of the ratchet woman's home-the one who lived right next door-the one God was asking her to tell about His love.

For the life of her, Lori couldn't make sense of how anyone could play such loud and obnoxious music so early in the morning. She had called the authorities on numerous occasions, but their presence didn't seem to deter her next-door neighbors from turning up the volume.

Lori had even tried to get the neighborhood council involved in the matter, but none of the other neighbors seemed as bothered by the music as she was. Lori's blood boiled every morning…almost to the point of hatred. It didn't quite get that far solely because she was a good Christian woman and knew that it was wrong to hate.

Interestingly, the one thing Lori never did was have a conversation and respectfully ask her neighbor to turn the volume a little lower in the morning. She didn't take her as the civilized type who would appreciate or respect such a request.

Lori closed her eyes and pleaded with God for the hundredth time, "I've always done just what You've asked of me. But I can't do it this time. I can't minister to someone I just don't like."

There was no answer-all she heard was her neighbors' music.

Lori sucked her teeth and let out a loud sigh.

Five years ago, when Lori moved onto her tree-lined street in the Bella Grande gated community of Sherman Oaks, she was so happy for the peace and comfort of it all. Her home was like her own little Garden of Eden, before the whole snake thing. Everything was perfect. She turned her backyard into a sanctuary, complete with a waterfall, fireplace, and cushioned lawn chair. She paid top dollar to make sure everything was perfectly manicured. From the grass that stretched across her half acre lot, to the shrubs and lavender flowers she had planted all around. Red, orange, and white rose bushes, orchids, dandelions, and lilacs were neatly arranged throughout the yard. Everything looked like a page right out of Home and Garden magazine-a truth that made Lori feel rather proud. She really enjoyed sitting outside her home and communing with God each morning. That is until the couple next door moved in. Everything changed the day they arrived. The peace she had once known seemed to instantly disappear.

Lori had to push her devotional time from 6:15am to 6:00am in order to be completely finished and back inside her home before the 7:15am music began to play. Today she had lingered a little longer than she intended, hoping God would speak, but that hadn't happened. She was annoyed.

The day they moved in, Lori thought she would take them some fresh homemade cookies (and sneak a look around to see how they had decorated). To her surprise, a "plastic-looking" woman in short shorts and a halter top opened the door and greeted her. Although the woman may have been naturally pretty years ago, she had obviously had a few botched procedures that left her looking more like a cat than a woman. Lori stood just staring at her for a few beats before the woman asked a little more forcefully in an unmistakable Bostonian accent, "May I help you?"

"Hi. Yes. My name is Lori. I live next door," she said and pointed to her home. "I made some honey sweetened chocolate chip pistachio nut cookies to welcome you and your family to the neighborhood," she said in a cheery voice and offered her most pleasant smile.

"Oh no," the woman said with a frown, her face a ball of terror as she frantically shook her head. "My children and I are *severely* allergic to honey."

"I see," said Lori, the wind taken out of her sails. She lowered the bag of cookies and added, "*Severely* allergic? That's just horrible."

"Who is that, Beth," she heard a deep commanding voice yell from upstairs.

"No one important," Beth turned and yelled back.

No one important?

Without another word, Lori turned and made her way back to her own home-hurt, offended, and extremely upset. Beth never said goodbye, never apologized, nothing.

Every day after that initial meeting, Lori would look out her kitchen window, which was adjacent to their unkempt front yard, and burn with intense anger. Each day she noticed something that made her dislike them even more than she did the previous day.

For example, neither the husband nor the wife seemed to work. How could they afford the mortgage in Lori's bourgeois neighborhood along with the Porsche and Range Rover that sat in their driveway? The husband had to be in his late forties and still wore his pants below his waist. That was just tasteless. The children, a girl and a boy, who appeared to be between the ages of 12 and 16 spoke loud obscenities to one another when they talked outside. The son dressed in oversized clothes like his father, and the daughter in too short, too tight get-ups like her mother. It was evident the parents hadn't taught them anything about self-respect, appropriate attire, or manners.

At night, exotic cars with ethnic drivers bumping hip-hop music would pull up to their home. The husband would come out, an exchange would take place, and the driver would speed off. These were apparent drug deals. Lori's head constantly shook when her mind made it to her neighbors. Come to think of it, were they even married? Lori just went ahead and added shacking to the list of things she disliked about them-just because.

There was a huge part of her that wished she hadn't disclosed the honey in the cookies a year ago. And she disliked her neighbors even more for making her dislike them enough to wish such a horrible thing.

Lori went inside the back door, which led directly into the kitchen, and took a bottle of Arrowhead water out of her refrigerator. She had forty minutes to get to the morning meeting she had scheduled with Logan, whom she hired to spearhead her prison ministry. She had showered and dressed before her devotional time, since she knew she would need to leave immediately after. She walked through her living room, stroked and kissed her Siberian cat, Bertha, who was resting on Lori's suede couch, and picked up her keys and wallet. After locking her front door, she noticed the most adorable Goldendoodle standing near the trunk of her car. She had never seen this dog before and figured he must be lost. She instantly fell in love with him because he looked very similar to the one she had as a young girl. His tongue hung happily and he wagged his tail as he stood on his hind legs.

"Hi cutie pie," Lori said as she stooped to rub his head. The dog immediately grabbed her wallet with his teeth.

"Bad boy," Lori playfully chided. Give me that," she said.

The dog took a few steps backward and then turned and trotted.

Lori stood in disbelief for a split second before she realized what had happened.

"Come back here," she demanded and went after him.

The Goldendoodle began to run.

Lori ran after him.

He ran to the end of the block, crossed the street, ran to the other end of the block, turned around and kept on running. Lori followed, but she was unable to keep up. Her years as a high school track star were long gone. She made a note to start doing cardio next week after her prayer time.

"This isn't funny, buddy. Give me that," she said as she ran panting behind him.

This went on for a few minutes before Lori looked up and realized that the dog had led her, wallet in teeth, right into the gate of the home next door to her own-the one where the deplorable woman lived! She could hear the music pulsating through the walls. The dog walked right up to the front porch and scratched the door with his paws. Lori was close behind pleading for him to give the wallet to her.

The music stopped and a few seconds later, the front door swung open. The Goldendoodle dropped Lori's wallet just behind Beth, who stood looking surprised by the scene happening in front of her.

All the color drained from Lori's face and she felt faint-maybe it was from the hopeless minutes she had spent running after the Goldendoodle…or maybe it was from the irony of being face to face with the assignment she was running from.

"Sorry about that," Beth said, seemingly apologetic. "We're keeping Coltrane for a friend. I didn't even realize he had gotten out."

"Figures," Lori thought as she wondered who in their right mind would ask Beth to babysit their dog. There had to be a law against leaving your dog with someone like her.

Beth bent down to pick up Lori's wallet and handed it to her.

"It's alright," Lori said, feeling extremely uncomfortable and short of breath.

"Lori, right?"

"Yes."

"Well I'm very happy to see you," she said and smiled, her cat-like features more welcoming than Lori remembered them a year ago.

Lori returned Beth's smile, only she was sure her own didn't look genuine.

"Please come inside and have a cup of coffee with me," Beth said. "Darren and the kids will be leaving for school and work in a sec."

"I would love to," Lori lied, "But I was actually-"

Before she could finish her sentence, her cell phone buzzed. She looked at the text from Logan. He had had an emergency and needed to reschedule their meeting.

Lori looked up at Beth's inquisitive eyes and wondered what she should do. She hadn't had the desire to sit and sip with Beth, but God had taken away her excuses and even placed her exactly where she was sure He wanted her to be.

After a long sigh and with a shake of her head, Lori said disappointedly, "Well it looks like I'll be able to have that drink of coffee after all. My appointment just cancelled."

"Great," Beth smiled. "Please follow me."

Lori glanced around to see whether any of her neighbors were outside to see her going into Beth's house, but the street was as empty as it had been when she chased Coltrane. She stepped inside the foyer and noticed it was decorated simply, yet beautifully. All the furniture in the great room was either white or dark cherry wood. It was so rich looking-the best drug money could buy, Lori guessed. White marble floors accentuated white columns that stretched to the nine foot ceiling. Sky lights overhead lit the massive room with the beautiful natural sunlight of May's splendor. Seeing Beth and her family outside Lori never would have guessed that the inside of their home was so prim and proper.

"This way," Beth said and pointed toward a sunroom at the rear of the house. "I'll get you a bottle of water too. You seem a little winded. I apologize again for Coltrane. I can't believe he took your wallet. He's usually so well-behaved when he's with us. I'm not sure what got into him this morning."

Lori knew exactly what had gotten into him. He too had an assignment-one that he had successfully completed.

Just then Lori remembered Beth's husband. Was it dangerous for her to be inside their home? After all she had already convinced herself that they were involved in illegal activities.

"Don't be afraid. Just tell her," she felt the Spirit stir within her. God's persistence in this moment assured her that regardless of Beth's husband's occupation, she didn't have anything to worry about. God would protect her.

As they walked through the living room, Lori noticed family portraits hanging along the walls. The children looked distinguished, the husband regal, and Beth, strikingly beautiful-much different than the collagen injected woman who walked ahead of her.

"Very nice portraits," Lori commented.

"Oh thank you. My father painted those shortly before he passed away."

"Simply beautiful."

"Yeah," Beth sighed. "Things were a lot different back then. His death took a real toll on us," Beth said with evident sorrow. "We actually moved here right after he passed. I was depressed for a while after that. I mean I had to take medication and everything. It was so hard."

"I'm sorry for your loss," Lori offered sincerely. "I lost my dad when I was in college, and I was beyond devastated," she said remembering the horrible turn her life had taken after his death. Thankfully God sent someone to tell Lori about Him and the peace she would find in Him. And thankfully, Lori accepted His offer and allowed Him to heal her broken heart and change her life. She decided to follow Him and her life had never been the same. She let out a sigh.

Noticing the platinum records that hung along the wall, Lori couldn't help but ask, "Are you a musician?"

Beth smiled. "Those are my husband's. He's a producer. He's worked with some of the biggest names in the music industry."

"A producer?" Lori asked.

"Yes," Beth said. "He owns a studio in Hollywood, but he has a studio here too. Sometimes he does last minute touch-ups in the morning before he drops the kids off at school and heads to work."

Lori nodded her head, finally understanding the reason behind the morning mayhem.

When they made it to the sunroom, Beth invited Lori to have a seat and she headed into the kitchen. Lori could hear Beth's husband and children walk down the steps leading into the foyer and out the front door. No one said goodbye, but a few seconds later she heard their car start and pull off. Beth returned with two cups of coffee and a bottle of water on a wooden tray. She set the tray down in front of Lori and smiled.

"It must be fate-you standing outside my door this morning," Beth said as she took a sip of her black coffee.

"Tell me about it," Lori thought as she stirred two spoons full of sugar and creamer into her own.

"I invited you in because there's something I've been wanting to talk to you about," Beth confessed.

Lori took a sip of her coffee, which was actually some of the best she had ever tasted, and wondered what Beth was referring to. If this was about the visits from the police, Lori was prepared to deny her involvement in the matter.

Beth continued, "I noticed you get dressed up on Sunday mornings and I assume that you are headed to church."

Lori nodded.

"Well I've never been one to go to church. I'm not really the religious type."

Lori nodded. She could tell that much.

"I mean, don't get me wrong. I believe in a Higher Power. I just don't know what to do with that belief, ya know?"

Lori nodded knowingly and took another sip of her delicious coffee. She still didn't want to deliver God's message. It was evident that Beth was ready to hear it, but Lori had spent so much time loathing her that the thought of delivering a message about God's love and Beth's possibly giving her heart right back to Him was a bridge that she herself wasn't ready to cross.

"Tell her," Lori felt the Holy Spirit speak into her heart. She took another sip of coffee and set it back on the table.

Lori remained silent.

"When my father passed away it made me think a lot about the point of it all. It made me question whether death is really the end of it all. My dad was a strong Christ follower and right before he died, I could see the most peaceful look on his face. I knew he had to have been in pain, but all I saw was peace. That's what I want. I want to feel that same peace."

Lori could relate. That was what she longed for when her own father had passed away. God was the only One who offered that peace. She could see the longing on Beth's face. Lori's heart softened.

"I completely understand," Lori said.

Just then Beth's cell phone rang. She looked at it, apologized that she would have to take the call, and walked into the kitchen.

Coltrane sauntered into the room, tail wagging happily behind him. He barked and walked over to Lori. Lori rubbed his back and the dog rested at her feet. Today had been the first time she had audibly heard from God in two weeks. She was happy that He had spoken to her again and now she finally understood why He had given her this assignment.

"God you're something else," Lori thought.

"Tell her," was His response.

A minute later, Beth walked back in the room and apologized again.

"That was my son. He forgot his project so I'm going to take it to him before his lunch break. These kids nowadays," she commented and shook her head.

"I know," Lori agreed. "They're a direct reflection of their parents," she added and took another sip of coffee.

Beth didn't seem to notice the jab and Lori immediately regretted saying it.

"Anyway, back to what I was saying. I was hoping you could tell me a little about what *you* believe. I've been watching you for months and I can tell that you're the real deal. I want to know more about God, but I don't know where to start. I don't just want to walk into a random church and find out it's a cult or something. It's sad to say that I don't have a single friend I can talk to about this. They'd call me crazy if they knew I wanted to know more about God."

Lori shook her head at the thought. She completely understood the feeling.

Beth continued, "I've been wanting to talk to you for a couple weeks now, but I couldn't quite pull myself to do it. I'm happy you showed up today. I mean, I'm sorry about the whole wallet thing, but I'm happy you're here."

Lori felt an overwhelming feeling of guilt. Beth seemed to have a sincere desire to hear about the One Lori loved the best. Lori's whole purpose for being on this earth, she knew, was to evangelize-to tell the lost about the Savior. Lori traveled the world sharing her faith in Christ, but she had failed to see the brokenness and need of the woman who lived right next door-a woman whose story was reminiscent of her own. Lori hadn't spoken to her or shown her the love of God since their initial meeting. She hadn't thought one kind thought about her before today. She was ashamed.

"Enough self-pity. Tell her," this time His voice was more firm than it had ever been. A tear rolled down Lori's cheek. She took a deep breath and a sip of water and delivered the message God had placed on her heart two weeks ago.

"Well it's funny you say that you've wanted to talk with me for a couple weeks now because a couple weeks ago God actually told me to deliver a very important message to *you*. I know that might sound a little strange, but that's the type relationship we have."

Beth looked shocked. "Really? That must be amazing," she said.

"It really is," Lori confirmed and continued. "During my prayer time a few weeks ago, He told me to come here and tell you that He loves you. Quite honestly I didn't know how you would take that. I didn't want to deliver that message and I hadn't actually planned on doing it."

Beth looked confused.

"Long story," Lori said. Someday she'd share it, but that wasn't her purpose today.

Lori proceeded to tell her about her own testimony-how she had come to know God, how she had first experienced His great love for her, and how His love had changed her life and revealed her purpose.

The words came much more easily than she had expected them to and Beth received them all much better than Lori had imagined she would.

Beth was obviously full of emotions. "I'm just so happy," she cried. "You don't know how wonderful that makes me feel. I can feel His presence right now as we speak," Beth said through sobs.

"I can too," Lori agreed and gave Beth a side hug. Beth rested her head on Lori's shoulder and they both looked out at Beth's yard, which also looked like a page ripped from a gardening magazine. From the condition of Beth's front yard, Lori never imagined that the back would be nearly as well manicured as it was. Lori was happy that she had finally gotten over herself and completed her assignment.

Suddenly she thought about the story of Jonah and how God had told him to go to Nineveh and deliver a message. Jonah hadn't wanted to go. He had tried to run from God's assignment, but God allowed him to be swallowed up by a whale, where he spent the three days it took the whale to get him to Nineveh. On the third day the whale spit him out on dry land and Jonah reluctantly delivered God's warning to the Ninevites. Like Beth, they wholeheartedly received God's message and it changed their lives. The difference in this case was, as Lori realized, she was actually happy to see God move in Beth's life.

Lori was overjoyed at the thought of Beth sharing the message with her husband and her children and seeing them all live new meaningful lives in Him. Lori knew that God's love would change their lives, as it had her own many years ago. She even hoped God would allow her to be part of their journey. While she sat hugging Beth, she promised God that from then on *whatever* He asked of her, her answer would be an immediate yes. She didn't have to understand or like His request. His plan is perfect. All she had to do was obey and trust Him to handle the rest.

Home of the Dons

"We are all brothers under the skin - and I, for one, would be willing to skin humanity to prove it."

-Ayn Rand

Sarah sat in the front center seat and nervously sipped a Starbucks non-coffee Frappuccino. It was 7:45am and she was among the first to arrive to Mrs. Richard's eleventh grade American Literature class. She noticed a shy looking black girl in the front row on the opposite side of the room. The girl was dressed plainly in no-name blue jeans and a pink shirt that appeared to have been bought at Target. She wore thick eyeglasses, a head full of twists, and a serious face that was buried in a thick book with a picture of Malcom X on the cover.

She must have noticed Sarah staring at her because she looked up from her book and gave her a look that clearly said, "Quit staring at me, or else." Sarah smiled and waved to let her know that she hadn't meant any harm. The girl rolled her eyes and continued reading.

Well, she's rude, Sarah thought.

Sarah looked at her phone. 7:50a.m. Where was everyone? So far there were only three people present-the rude black girl on the other side of the room, an overweight boy dressed in black in the back of the room, and Sarah. She wondered what the rest of the class would be like and played a few rounds of Temple Run to calm her nerves.

This was Sarah's first day at Dorsey High School-Home of the Dons. Her father decided to open a laundry business in a minority community, and chose the Crenshaw District as the perfect location. He found a reasonably priced home in Baldwin Hills, which was approximately 3 minutes from Dorsey and 4 minutes from her father's Laundromat.

When Sarah's father first told her that they would be moving, she was extremely sad. It had taken her all of six months to *finally* begin to fit in at her old school, Valley Prep. She hated to leave behind her teachers and friends. She had heard rumors about Dorsey, and was scared of going to school there and living so close to the notorious Jungle. She heard that many of the African Americans on that side of town still blamed Caucasians for their poor living conditions and general dissatisfaction with life.

She hoped the kids in her class would be able to see that she wasn't the average valley white girl. She hoped they could look beyond the color of her skin and accept her for who she was.

Sarah glanced at the clock once again. 7:52 a.m. There were still only three people in the room. Where was the instructor? This was nothing like Valley Prep, where at 7:45 a.m., all the students and teachers assumed their positions at their desks. Sarah knew that Mrs. Richard *had* to be at school because the classroom door was open when she arrived at 7:30 a.m., and there was a Credit Union bag sitting on the desk. The words "First Period American Literature" were written on the dry-erase board along with the teacher's name.

Maybe there weren't many students in class yet because they were operating on "C.P. time." Sarah had heard that African Americans were rarely on time because they followed a time schedule all their own. To them, 7:00 meant 7:10, and so on. Sarah hated to think of herself as a person who believed in stereotypes, but it did seem kind of strange that by 7:52 a.m. only three people were at their desks. She wondered whether the late bell rang at "real time" 8 o'clock or "C.P. time" 8 o'clock.

Sarah pulled out her Bebe pocket mirror and looked herself over one more time. She hadn't worn her best clothes because she wanted to scope out the school and see what other students had on first. She didn't want to show up over-dressed and be made fun of, nor did she want to show up under-dressed and be made fun of. She decided to dress comfortably in dark blue denim shorts she bought from Forever 21, a yellow H&M shirt, and blue and yellow Ked's. She wore her long auburn hair in a high bun and a little blue eye shadow and Mac lip gloss. She placed her mirror in her backpack and scrolled through her Instagram feed.

At 7:55 a.m. students began entering the class in groups. They were talking to and laughing with one another. It seemed as though all of them had been friends for years. Sarah wondered whether there was a place for her in their cliques. She noticed guys who were obviously athletes, girls who were probably cheerleaders, and those who were likely considered nerds (like the rude black girl in front). Almost everyone in the class was Black, except for five Chicano students, who seemed to be part of a clique all by themselves. They sat on the far side of the classroom near the window, behind the rude Black girl.

Watching the students as they entered the room, Sarah tried to make eye contact with them and smile. It seemed to her, however, that she was invisible to them. She felt isolated-alone. Sarah missed Valley Prep.

7:58 a.m.

She heard a male voice behind her mockingly say, "Hey, check out Britney Spears in the front." Then there were numerous snickers. She glanced over her shoulder and noticed he was referring to her.

A female voice responded, "Looks like someone got out of the limo at the wrong school. Hey Britney. This is Dorsey. I think you must be lost." There was more laughter.

Sarah didn't respond. She sunk down in her chair, face forward, and shielded her eyes with her manicured hand. Sarah could feel herself turning red. Why couldn't her dad do business like a *normal* businessman? He didn't have to move to "the hood" to have a business there. They could have stayed in Granada Hills and he still could have had a successful laundry business in the Crenshaw District. Her feet began to twitch beneath her desk. Where was Mrs. Richard?

Sarah felt a tap on her shoulder but she didn't turn around.

"Don't pay them any attention," a female voice behind her whispered. "They're ignorant."

Sarah turned around and smiled at her. "Thanks," she said.

"So what *is* your name?" the girl asked.

"Sarah."

"Nice to meet you Sarah. My name is Bloushaquanisha Coolioquisha Pone Pone."

Sarah's mouth dropped and she blinked excessively. She had heard about Black people having "ghetto names" but had never actually met someone with a name *this* ghetto. At Valley Prep the most "ghetto" name she'd had to learn was Jamesetta. It was easy to remember and pronounce.

"I'm just kidding," the girl laughed. "My name is Lauren," she said and extended her hand.

Sarah giggled, relieved, and extended her hand as well. "Nice to meet you, Lauren."

"Hey Britney, why do all white girls drink Starbucks?" the same male heckler from the back of the room called out.

Laughter filled the room. Sarah was beyond embarrassed.

"Her name is Sarah, and that's not funny," Lauren shot back.

Sarah couldn't believe that Lauren had taken up for her so soon after meeting her.

A few people made kissy noises behind them.

"You's a good little house nigger, ain't you Lauren," the same female voice called out from the rear. The hecklers laughed and at that moment the tardy bell rang. 8:01 a.m. The bell really did ring on "C.P. time," Sarah thought as she glanced at her iPhone.

"That's enough, class," the rude Black girl in the front row said authoritatively. She set down her Malcom X novel, walked to the front of the classroom, and smiled apologetically at Sarah. Sarah hadn't noticed it earlier but from this angle she could tell that the rude Black girl was in her late twenties or early thirties-not a student at all. The class quieted down. The silence was uncomfortable.

"Young man in the back, what is your name?"

"Chris," he replied nervously.

"Well Chris and everyone else, my name is Mrs. Richard."

Sarah was shocked. Mrs. Richard had witnessed all the hoopla. She liked her already.

"This is my first year here at Dorsey. I have tons of friends who are proud Dorsey alumni. They say great things about this school but I must say I am quite disappointed in the behavior I observed here this morning. I think it is important we go over the class rules before we proceed. Please take out a sheet of paper and a pen," Mrs. Richard instructed.

The students shuffled to position their paper and pens for notes.

Mrs. Richard wrote the word RESPECT on the dry-erase board.

"Chris, what does this word say?"

"RESPECT."

"Everyone please write that word on your paper. The first rule is that we ALWAYS RESPECT ONE ANOTHER. That means the unkind comments and behavior we witnessed this morning are NEVER acceptable in this classroom. Chris, please come up here and apologize to Sarah and the rest of the class for your disrespectful behavior."

As Chris slowly made his way to the front of the classroom Mrs. Richard addressed the female heckler.

"Young lady in the back, what is your name?"

"Rachel."

"Please come to the front of the class and stand next to Chris."

Rachel walked to the front of the class.

"Rachel, I would like for you to apologize to Sarah, Lauren, and the rest of the class for your disrespectful behavior."

"Sorry," they both said in unison and looked at the floor.

Perhaps they were good actors, but to Sarah they truly looked remorseful. Sarah nodded at them and smiled.

"You two may have a seat," Mrs. Richard said.

Chris and Rachel returned to their seats.

Lauren tapped Sarah on the shoulder and they shared a quick smile.

"I see quite a few African American faces in this room. And we all know that our people have historically been mistreated solely because of our skin color. Knowing the effect that has had on us and our community, we should NEVER treat any other ethnic group with the same malice and disrespect. That is never ok. Some of you feel like you didn't do anything wrong because all you did was laugh at the foolishness that Chris and Rachel said. But if you laughed, you are guilty. I challenge you to be leaders. If something is wrong, have guts enough to stand alone, if necessary, and say that it is wrong. Do you all understand?"

"Yes," the class answered.

Sarah glanced back at Lauren again and smiled.

"Rule number two. Do not EVER use profanity in this classroom. Write that down and put a note next to it that says if I ever hear you use the N-word or any other derogatory term like it I will personally work to have you kicked out of this school. I am forgiving Rachel's indiscretion today because it is the first day and I hadn't made you aware of the rules before she said it, but if it happens again there won't be forgiveness. Understand?"

"Yes," many students responded. The rest nodded their heads.

Mrs. Richard wrote a few more rules on the board and for the next forty minutes she talked about her expectations of the class, different literature they would cover, and practical applications for her literary choices.

Sarah hoped the rest of her teachers were as awesome as she could already tell Mrs. Richard was.

At 8:51 a.m. the bell rang signaling the end of first period. Students shuffled to pack up their bags and Mrs. Richard dismissed the class.

Rachel rolled her eyes at Sarah and Lauren on her way out the door. Sarah wondered why she had such a chip on her shoulder. On Chris's way out the door, he turned and said in a hushed voice, "Sorry again, Britney."

"My name is Sarah," she corrected him.

"Right. Sarah. I'm sorry for giving you a hard time. I was just messing with you. You're alright with me," he said and held out his fist for dap.

Sarah nodded and gave him dap before he turned to walk out the door.

"So what do you have next?" Lauren asked and stood to leave

"P.E. with Coach Nash."

"He's real cool. Cute too. You'll love his class," she said blushing. "I'm headed that way so I'll walk over with you."

"Cool."

On their way out, Sarah stopped by Mrs. Richard's desk to thank her for what she had done.

"No problem. I'm sorry you had to experience that. This is a great school. Things are going to be just fine for you. I'm sure of it."

Sarah smiled. "I hope you're right," she said.

She and Lauren exited the classroom and headed for the P.E. field. The hallways were crowded with Black and Chicano students. Sarah had never seen anything like it. She felt like she was on display as she walked through the hallway, but thankfully she was greeted by pleasant faces. Sarah smiled. Perhaps it wouldn't be so bad here after all. And she had already made one new friend.

Alumni Night at Chekhov

"Don't dream your life. Live your dream."

-Miasha

"To thine own self be true."

-William Shakespeare

Tara

Tara stared at her blank computer screen with motionless fingers positioned above its home keys. The smooth melodies of Keiko Matsui pulsated through her headphones, lingering in her ears as she re-read the prompt: *"To thine own self be true." Write a story exploring the charge given to Laertes by Polonius.*

Tara hadn't written a single line worth keeping and the assignment was due in two days. To make matters worse, the production phase of *The Crucible* was well underway. Tara had to be at Chekhov's School of the Arts five days a week instead of the normal two. Luckily, she'd been able to talk herself into the assistant director role this year, which meant less pressure to memorize lines and her first AD credit. But it also meant that her mother, Deirdre, who prided time spent on stage above all else, would be very unhappy when she found out.

Tara sighed.

Usually listening to music and gazing out her bedroom window at gigantic homes across the waterfront inspired her to write tales of pampered housewives, spoiled teenagers, rambunctious attorneys, and the like. She could easily knock out a five page narrative in a few hours. But this time was different. She wanted to write something more-

Honest.

But what?

"Tara, can you explain to me why it is 8:15 and you are still in your pajamas?"

Tara jumped, her heart racing at the sound of her mother's raised voice so close to her. Despite Tara's numerous requests, Deirdre refused to knock on her bedroom door. "My house. My rules," her mother often reminded her.

Tara glanced at the digital clock on the nightstand next to her bed. She hurriedly closed her empty Word document and removed her headphones.

"I lost track of time," she said as she pulled her shoulder-length tresses into the rubber band she wore on her wrist. "I just need two minutes," she said and scurried toward her closet to change.

"A person who is serious about her craft never loses track of time, Tara. That is unacceptable."

Tara hated that she had given her mother reason to remind her of this again.

"Yes, mother," Tara replied, the closet shielding her from Deirdre's always-piercing eyes.

If Tara were anything like the characters in the stories she wrote, she would get in her mother's face, tell her that she no longer wanted to act, and threaten to run away.

But she wasn't like them.

Tara stuffed pink ballet shoes into her purple drawstring bag and pulled out the invitation for the Alumni Night at Chekhov. She weighed her options while Deirdre continued her tirade on the other side of the closet doors. If Tara gave the invitation to her mother, she was sure Deirdre would want to go. That would put Tara one step further from finishing her homework that night. But on the other hand, it would stop Deirdre's ranting.

"Oh mom," Tara interrupted, handing the invitation to her. "I forgot to give this to you last week."

Deirdre studied it for a few beats and then smiled bigger than Tara had seen in months.

"Did you see this, sweetheart? 'Alumni Night at Chekhov. Current and Former Students Only.'"

"Yeah. I thought you'd be pretty excited," Tara said pleased with her seamless subject change.

Twenty years earlier, Deirdre graced the corridors as a student at Chekhov, the most respected school of the arts for adolescents on the West Coast. It produced more professional thespians than any other training facility in the world. Only the talented were accepted and only the extremely talented made it into productions. The fact that Deirdre had a starring role each of the five years she was there attested to her dexterity. Old videos and newspaper clippings confirmed it and she made sure to tout her accomplishments regularly.

"Wait a minute," panic seemed to sweep across Deirdre's mocha face. Her dark almond eyes widened causing the creases in her forehead to upstage her flawless skin. "This is tonight? Why are you just now giving this to me?"

"I completely forgot about it after class last week," Tara replied, hoping to sound remorseful.

It was true. She *had* forgotten immediately after class and then chose not to mention it when it crossed her mind the many times after that.

Tara felt uncomfortable as Deirdre's coal eyes seemed to indict her. *Was she buying this?*

After a pregnant pause, Deirdre finally said softly, "No big deal."

Tara exhaled.

"But for the record, this is yet another example of you being irresponsible. This is unacceptable. Next time a paper is sent home for me, give it to me immediately. Do you understand? Because I'm tired of repeating myself."

"Yes, mother," Tara answered, looking at the plush lavender rug beneath her to avoid those fiery eyes.

Three years ago when Tara told her mother she wanted to follow in her footsteps, Deirdre jumped all over it. She gave Tara a complete makeover: new wardrobe, bi-monthly hair appointments, and laser acne treatments. Deirdre even had Traung Nguyen, celebrity photographer, take overpriced headshots of Tara. Deirdre enrolled her at Chekhov before Tara could mention that she'd changed her mind.

"So, I guess I'll wear my burgundy heels and that black dress I wore to the ballet last month. What do you think?" Deirdre asked, her excitement seeming to return.

Tara thought it would be too revealing for an event with teenagers.

"That will be cute," she shrugged.

"Perfect. What are you going to wear?"

"What I have on now," Tara said as she ran her hands across her black Chekhov uniform tank and gray sweats.

She had rolled the bottoms of her sweats up and thrown on a pair of black Chucks. She wore the diamond studs her mother had given her on her fourteenth birthday. Simple. Comfortable. Fitting.

Deirdre looked frowningly at Tara. "Oh absolutely not! You never know who will be at these events. You have to dress for success at all times. Make yourself stand out above the others. Did I ever tell you about the time

I met the French director Madame Toussaint at the Beverly Center?"

ONLY A THOUSAND TIMES, Tara screamed on the inside.

"I think so. You performed a scene for her right on the spot, correct?"

"Exactly. And all because I was never caught off guard. I never had to get ready because I stayed ready for whatever opportunities I happened upon. That's how you should be. Take that cute black sweater I just bought you. You can throw on a Spanx with it and you'll be picture perfect."

"Sure thing."

Tara headed back into the closet, eyes rolling, and stuffed a sweater and pair of dark blue jeans into her bag. At 5' 4" and 99 pounds, Tara didn't think she was anywhere near overweight, but Deirdre constantly insinuated that she was- another reason Tara was uninterested in acting professionally. She detested the emphasis placed on physical appearance.

Tara glanced at her watch as she emerged from her closet. 8:31.

"Ok, Mom. I'm ready when you are."

"Alright," Deirdre said as she headed towards Tara's bedroom door. "I'll grab my bag and meet you out front."

Deirdre brushed her fingers across the clapboard that hung on Tara's wall on her way out.

Alone, Tara looked around her bedroom. "Dream," "Lights. Camera. Action," and "Superstar" were stenciled in purple and hot pink all over her light gray walls. She looked at the director's chair and lighted full-length mirror across from her bed, her deflated reflection urging her to take a seat. She looked away, grabbed the iPod off her heart-shaped computer desk, and walked out the door to meet her mother.

***

Deirdre

Deirdre caught a glimpse of her reflection as she walked through Chekhov's glass doors. *Perfection.* The makeup artist at Nordstrom had done an amazing job accentuating her natural look with hints of plum and soft pink. Her jet black shoulder length Brazilian wavy wig drew attention to her bold cheeks, energetic eyes, Greek nose, and plump lips. Her low-cut black dress stopped mid-thigh and hugged her tightly. Burgundy stilettos heightened her Pilates-toned calves. Deirdre smiled, revealing impeccable pearl teeth and sauntered into the large foyer like a seasoned performer.

The pop sounds of Tyler Lovett's "Shake Your Body" pumped through wall-embedded speakers. On the brick wall opposite the entrance a rectangular banner reading "Welcome to Alumni Night" hung comfortably between posters of Chekhov's most recent alumni to hit the silver screen. A long rectangular table was loaded with fruit and vegetable platters, pepperoni pizzas, and bottled water. A small round table next to it held plates and napkins.

Deirdre glanced at her Tiffany watch. 6:56. She was the first one to arrive.

Deirdre walked along the saffron wall to the right of the entrance. 8X10s of its famous alumni hung along it. In picture after picture, Deirdre observed the smiling faces of those who had accomplished that which she herself had not.

She imagined Tara's picture hanging on the wall and smiled proudly.

At 6:58, students streamed through the French doors that led from the inner halls of Chekhov into the foyer. A few students quickly signed out at the receptionist's desk and continued through the front doors to meet their waiting parents. The majority of students stayed to enjoy the alumni celebration.

Deirdre listened in as a group of tweens talked about how much they hated Ms. Gracie's ballet class and couldn't understand why dance was even a part of the Chekhov curriculum. Just as Deirdre was about to interject her thoughts about the importance of being well-rounded, she spotted Tara.

Deirdre noted how similar she and Tara looked and shook her head. Tara had so much potential, but lacked the key ingredient to a successful acting career--drive. If there was some way to infuse just a portion of her own ambition into Tara's personality, her daughter would be unstoppable. There had to be a way.

"Hey darling. How was class?" Deirdre asked after giving Tara two cheek kisses and looking attentively into her eyes.

"It was cool."

"Well I see I'm the first alumnus to arrive," Deirdre commented as she looked around the studio and swept a piece of side bang behind her ear.

"Maybe they are trying to make an entrance," Tara offered.

"Chekhov alumni know better. Entrances should be made 'on time.' Being tardy is unacceptable. Remember that. Someone who is extremely talented but late could easily lose her role to someone who is less talented but on time. Do you understand?"

"Yes, mother," Tara replied.

Deirdre studied her watch again.

"Well, it's only 7:05. I'm sure they'll be here soon. Are you hungry?"

"Starving."

As they walked toward the food table, Deirdre reminded Tara that pizza was not an option for her.

"Your body is your instrument. If you're serious about this business, you have to keep it on pointe," Deirdre said.

"Ok," Tara said dryly.

Deirdre noticed the young thespians in attendance were all dressed in their Chekhov uniforms. She considered encouraging Tara to change back into hers in case of photo ops and then reasoned that standing out wasn't a bad alternative to fitting in.

By 7:30 Deirdre had briefly chatted with Tara's friends and after surveying the room again, noticed that everyone was under 21 with the exception of Madame Broussard, the office assistant and event chaperone.

Deirdre continued to scope the room and smiled when Mr. Chekhov, living legend, emerged from his office. A black t-shirt and black slacks clung to his small frame. Deirdre had never seen him with hair, but his eyebrows showed that he was once a redhead. Layers of bags beneath his tired green eyes reminded her of production days twenty years earlier.

"Mr. Chekhov!" Deirdre exclaimed and made her way over to him with Tara tagging behind. "It is so great to see you."

"Deena!" he exclaimed and opened his arms for an embrace.

"Deirdre," she corrected and stooped for a hug.

"Ah, yes. Deirdre. You look fabulous, as always." His New York accent was as thick now as it had been when Deirdre was a student.

"Thank you," she blushed.

"I guess Miss Tara here told you that she's our A.D. this year?"

Stunned, Deirdre glanced at Tara, whose eyes were glued to the hardwood floors beneath.

"Tara hadn't mentioned that to me."

"Well I'm honored to have her helping me out," Mr. Chekhov said. He smiled and placed his arm around Tara.

Tara continued to look at the floor.

"So do you have *any* lines, Tara?" Deirdre asked uneasily.

Tara didn't respond.

Deirdre looked to Mr. Chekhov for the answer.

"I wanted her gorgeous face on stage. You know she's one of our best. But she insisted on working behind the scenes. I figure her youthful eye can give an old work new perspective," Mr. Chekhov said as he nudged Tara and smiled.

"I see," Deirdre said trying to make sense of what she'd heard. She could feel her temperature rising and sighed disappointedly. How could Tara expect to gain respect as an actor if she wasn't acting?

"So, what brings you by this evening?" Mr. Chekhov asked.

"I'm here for Alumni Night, although it appears I'm the only one who got the memo." She let out a nervous laugh.

Mr. Chekhov looked at her and blinked profusely.

"Oh my. I told Madame Broussard that the invitations were unclear. Oh Deena, when we said alumni, we meant some of the teen stars from our past productions who are currently on the silver screen-Barry Mongory, Tabitha Hicks, Elissa Kraftsman."

Deirdre could feel the color drain from her face as she looked again at the posters hanging on the wall-posters of the three special guests. She thought about all the attention she had put into looking stellar and felt foolish. Deirdre could feel the familiar lump rising up in her throat.

"Don't get me wrong, we love that you are here. I just feel terrible that--"

"It's fine, Mr. Chekhov," Deirdre managed to say. "Really. Maybe I can make myself useful and help out with the refreshments or something."

"You know, mom," Tara interrupted, "I feel a little sick. If you don't mind, I'd like to just go," Tara said, red cheeked.

Deirdre examined Tara's face, her own, but distinctly different. Their silence spoke volumes and for the first time she saw the unhappiness in Tara's eyes.

"That's fine, dear. Whatever you want."

She turned back to Mr. Chekhov and extended her hand, "This is a great event. You really do such amazing work."

"Thank you. And again, I apologize for the mix-up." Mr. Chekhov turned his attention to Tara, "I hope you feel better," he said. He held her at arms' length and winked.

"Thanks, Mr. Chekhov."

As Deirdre and Tara made their way to the door, excitement erupted as Barry Mongory and his entourage entered. The sound of flashing cameras sickened Deirdre. Irrepressible tears blurred her vision. The cold air violently accosted her as she pushed out onto Avenue of the Stars, the "Die Hard" building in her peripheral. Traffic zoomed by and Deirdre felt the evening's weight consume her.

Deirdre looked at Tara, who also had tears in her eyes, and embraced her only child warmly. Deirdre closed her eyes and, as the tears flowed, accepted what she had denied for so long--her denouement.

In the Stall

"The kids who need the most love will ask for it in the most unloving ways."

-Unknown

I hear schools in the ritzy neighborhoods have really nice restrooms. The walls are clean. The toilets flush. Tush-friendly tissue flows freely and the sinks aren't packed with wadded up brown paper towels. I imagine they have classical music pumping through wall speakers and a little old lady standing next to the sink offering good smelling hand soap or lotion if you give her a portion of your lunch money. Peace. That's what I picture.

However, that's not at all the experience at Tubman Middle School. The walls are full of graffiti. The stall doors rarely lock and have all kinds of obscenities written across them. They always, without fail, from the time the morning bell rings until school lets out at 3pm, always, always smell like sewage-and for some reason the floors stay wet. I avoid the nastiness for the most part, but today I had a serious case of the BGs and it would've taken too long to get a note to use the one in the nurse's office-so I held my breath and went in.

I figured I might as well read the gossip on the door of my stall since I was in there and that's when I saw it: My name-first and last-tagged in blue Sharpie with the word "TRICK" written in bubble letters on top of it. If that wasn't bad enough, someone had drawn an unflattering picture of me right next to it. The drawing of me had crooked oversized glasses and way more freckles than I actually have. The ears looked like they belonged to Yoda and the artist laid the bags on pretty thick. To say I was pissed would be an understatement. I had to figure out who had done this so I could put my fist in their face or report them to the principle, depending on who it was. Because, let's just be real-there are a few chicks here you couldn't pay me all the money in the world to fight.

Back in Mrs. Baxter's English class I couldn't focus on a single word she said. My mind was still in the bathroom. I had to get a Sharpie of my own so I could scratch out the god-awful foolishness someone had written. And who was that *someone*?

"Daydreaming again, Clarissa?" Mrs. Baxter asked, standing right over me. She was swimming in floral perfume, which didn't do anything to help my upset stomach.

"Sorry Mrs. Baxter," I said for the hundredth time this school year.

"Pay attention. Everything I'm saying today *will* be on tomorrow's test."

"Yes ma'am." I nodded.

As soon as she walked away I went back to figuring this thing out.

I bet it was Teresa Hodgkins. I could tell she was jealous of me by the way she rolled her eyes whenever I looked at her. Plus, I heard she used to have a crush on Ronnie Atkins and he wasn't feeling her because he was super sprung on me.

Or maybe it was Candance Johnson. Word in the halls is her momma gave her that ghetto name hoping she would be able to dance. I honestly think she misspelled it on her birth certificate and then just rolled with it. Anyway, although she always smiled in my face, I could tell Candance was jealous of me because I got most of the solo parts in Modern.

Yeah. It had to be Teresa or Candance. I was going to get to the bottom of it.

As soon as the bell rang I grabbed a black Sharpie from Mrs. Baxter's desk and followed Teresa Hodgkins to her locker. She didn't seem to notice me until after she had entered her combination and opened it. She paused, turned around to look at me, sighed, and rolled her eyes.

"What?" She seemed annoyed-more annoyed than usual. That was a sign of guilt.

"Do you have a problem with me?" I demanded.

"What?"

"I heard you were talking about me behind my back," I lied.

"I don't care enough about you to have a problem with you. And if I had something to say about you I would say it to your face. Now please move, you goober."

The *dangs*, *ooohs* and *ahhhs* flooded the hallway as everyone in earshot laughed, shook their heads, and pointed in my direction.

I couldn't stand Teresa's ugly self!

I looked in her beetle eyes and returned her irritation with a little of my own. I can always tell when someone's lying because their eyes twitch if you stare at them hard enough. Her eyes were steel-cold, hard, and unmoving. It was obvious she was telling the truth. And to be honest, the way she spoke her truth stung a little.

Just for the heck of it I threw my shoulders at her as if I were going to punch.

She flinched.

I rolled my eyes and walked away.

"She told you," Norris Johnson said as I walked by.

"Shut up!" I shouted.

That set the hallway off again.

"Shut up," the childish idiots echoed as I stomped toward the bathroom. They made me so sick. I was hot. I couldn't wait for the semester to end so I could be outta this hell hole. I was so over middle school.

The smell of sewage accosted me even before I stepped foot in the bathroom. When I opened the door I noticed Tiffany Randle walking out of the stall that I had been in earlier. She looked nervously at me.

"Hey Clarissa."

"Hey."

When she saw that I was going into the stall she had just come out of she added, "It wasn't me."

I nodded my head. She was a nice girl. There's no way she had written it.

Tiffany walked out without washing her hands-so gross-and I headed into the rancid stall. When I closed the door my mouth hit the floor. Someone had added the word "Stupid" in front of the word "TRICK." I was livid. It hadn't even been an hour since I last left this stall. Nutrition had just started so unless someone had gotten a pass to leave second period, the person who wrote it must have come in here as soon as the bell rang. My mind went back to Candance. Her second period was across the hall so she had to have written it and left in the time it took me to get back here. I scratched out all the references to me and decided I would confront Candance during warm-ups next period.

I was in Mrs. Stevens' Modern class five minutes before the late bell rang. Mrs. Stevens always played old school R&B love songs for the first ten minutes, and since the music was already playing I figured I might as well prepare for the butt whipping I might have to unleash on Candance if she said the wrong thing. I rotated my head and arms and did lunges on each leg. I even swung at an imaginary punching bag and imagined I was Floyd Money.

Candance came sauntering in with her crew a few seconds after the tardy bell rang. When she saw me heading in her direction, she smiled and said sweetly, "Hey Clarissa. How's it going?"

"I need to speak to you for a second."

"What's up?" she asked.

I looked at her two friends and added, "Alone."

Her friends smacked their lips and walked to the other side of the room.

"What's up, Clarissa? Is everything alright?"

"Not really," I said with an attitude.

"What's going on?" she asked with what seemed like fake concern.

"Well I heard you wrote some messed up stuff about me on the wall in the bathroom," I lied.

Candance put her hand on her chest and with wide eyes said, "You're my *friend*. I would *never* do that."

I studied her for a moment. Something about the way she said "friend" and the coy way she batted her eyes when she said "never" let me know she was lying. I'm not sure what came over me, but the next thing I knew a flurry of my fists had landed on her face, chest, and stomach. She didn't stand a chance as I laid into her for all the drama I had been through over the last three years. Everything happened so fast, but I remember hearing her two friends scream and I know that someone pulled me off of her.

Suspended. I stared at the frosted barred window next to Principal Salaam's office and mulled over that word while I waited for my mother to pick me up. There's no doubt I was going to get a serious butt whipping myself tonight. My mom wouldn't care why I had done it. She never did. And the fact that she would have to take off work and figure out what to do with me for the next three days would make matters even worse.

My trance was broken when Tiffany Randle and her obviously upset father walked out of Principal Salaam's office and stood in front of the window. Tiffany's eyes were glued to the linoleum and Principal Salaam held a blue Sharpie in his hand.

"I apologize again for the inconvenience, Principal Salaam. Tiffany is going to have to work very hard to pay for all the walls she's written on. And trust me-this won't ever happen again, right Tiffany?"

Tiffany avoided their eyes and nodded her head.

"Thank you, Mr. Randle," Principal Salaam said as he twirled the Sharpie in his left hand.

I couldn't believe what I was hearing. It was as if time stood still. I looked at Tiffany and then back at the Sharpie. I burned a hole through Tiffany with my eyes and I swear she smirked when she glanced at me. I hadn't suspected her at all earlier and if I wasn't here right now watching all this, I would never believe that she had done such a thing. I had used so much of my energy fighting, I couldn't even muster up the anger I would ordinarily feel toward her. Instead, I was ashamed.

I replayed the moment right before the fight in my head. Candance had called me friend. In my three years at Tubman, there wasn't a single person who had ever called me that. Maybe that's why it was so hard to believe. And now that I knew Candance hadn't written that stuff, I could honestly say that she looked sincere when she said it. I'd screwed up. All I ever wanted was someone I could call my friend and I had beat up the one person who actually thought of me as such. I wondered if Candance could forgive me-whether there was any hope of us having a friendship. I sure hoped so.

The Visionary

"Vision is the art of seeing what is invisible to others."
-Jonathan Swift

"Pastor Gaines, with all due respect, there's no way we can afford to take this kind of risk," Deacon Clemmons said, the incandescent overhead lights reflecting off his bald head. Deacon Clemmons dabbed a handkerchief at the corners of his ample lips and added, "If we don't come up with the money to catch up our mortgage we'll be forced to shut our doors."

"I agree," Deacon Blake chimed in, his accent still Mississippi through and through, even though he had been in California the majority of his life. "The numbers don't add up. Instead of spending $2,500 that we don't have on a fundraiser, we need to use common sense and pay the bills that need to be paid. We have administrators who have been slaving for chicken scratch for years. We need to take care of them before we start dishing out money for fundraisers."

"I understand why you feel that way, but I've received clear instructions from God. What we're going to raise through this fundraiser will be enough to keep our doors open until Christ returns. And The Anointed Messengers have agreed to perform for free. That alone will draw a nice crowd," Pastor Gaines said confidently as he ran his hands over his shoulder-length sandy brown dreads. His jovial hazel eyes and smooth light brown skin gave the impression that he was younger than the 35 years he actually was. But the sound of his powerful voice and the conviction with which he always spoke made him wise beyond his years and able to lead a congregation comprised mostly of his elders.

"You're a big dreamer, Pastor. You've gotten the message wrong a few times in the past and the congregation has suffered," Deacon Clemmons reminded him.

Pastor Gaines thought for a moment. He had indeed gotten the message wrong a few times, usually on small things. But his biggest flop had occurred many years ago when he placed Dina, a recovering addict he met while volunteering at St. John's Drug & Psychiatric Treatment Center, in charge of depositing the church's weekly offerings. He thought it would encourage her to continue living for Christ, share her testimony with other recovering addicts, and spread the gospel good news. But after six months on the job, Pastor Gaines discovered she had forged his signature on multiple documents and nearly drained the church's bank accounts. The church racked up hefty legal fees undoing the damage she caused. She was later arrested for selling narcotics to an undercover officer and the congregation was extremely disappointed in their pastor for making such an irresponsible decision. But that was years ago. He still ministered at the center and hadn't come across another person whose conversion proved insincere.

"You're right, Deacon Clemmons. But I've grown over the past ten years. I know His voice when I hear it- and He wants us to have this fundraiser," the pastor responded assertively.

"Membership is at an all-time low, Pastor. Even if we have a fundraiser, there's no way we'll raise enough money on a monthly basis to keep the doors open permanently. What we really need is a plan to grow the congregation to the numbers we had when your father was pastor," Deacon Blake offered.

"Membership won't be a problem after the fundraiser," Pastor Gaines said firmly.

"How are you so sure?" asked Deacon Treadmore.

"God showed me a *vision* of our church breaking ground on an acre of land right here in Long Beach. There were people all around-people from every continent, different races, shapes, sizes, backgrounds-more than I could number. I felt peace in my spirit. Because, through this vision, God confirmed that He would bless Israel Christian Fellowship, as He did for Jabez and countless other faithful servants who obeyed Him."

"This is some kinda faith you have, Pastor," said Sis. Petunia as she smiled supportively at their leader.

"I've never been so sure of anything in my whole life," he assured her.

"Yeah. You might want to take the matter back to the Lord and let Him know you need Him to show you another plan-one that the deacons, deaconesses and trustees can see too," Deacon Clemmons said with a chuckle.

The others shook their heads and looked incredulously at the deacon.

"I need you all to trust me," Pastor Gaines said as he tensely tapped his fingers on the table, unamused by Deacon Clemmons' humor. "And if that is too difficult, trust that God has put me over this congregation and trust that He won't allow me to do anything that doesn't align with His will. Can you all just do that?"

"I'll do whatever I can to help, but I want the record to show that I opposed this move," Deacon Clemmons said.

"I respect your position and we have made note of it in the records," Pastor Gaines said. He paused for a moment and looked around at the church's board of directors. Their faces showed that they had heard enough and were ready to head home. Many of them had served in the same capacity when his father was pastor. He loved them because although they didn't always see eye to eye, there was no doubt in his mind that they genuinely cared about the church and its congregation. He trusted them to do what they felt was best and hoped that today the majority of them would be unlike Deacon Clemmons and take a leap of faith with him.

"Well I think we've all voiced our concerns," Pastor Gaines said. "Let's go ahead and take a vote. May I have a motion to move forward with the fundraiser?"

"I so move," Sis. Clemmons said, ignoring the stare of her husband.

"I second the motion," Deacon Treadmore said.

"It has been properly moved and seconded. All in favor, say I."

Eight "I's" echoed around the table. All but Pastor Gaines, who was unable to vote in business meetings, Deacon Clemmons and Deacon Blake. Pastor Gaines exhaled a sigh of relief. This road was not a smooth one, but at least he was one step closer to fulfilling his assignment.

"I's have it. And so declared," Pastor Gaines said. "Thank you all. This is going to be the best move in the history of Israel Christian Fellowship. Deacon Blake. Deacon Clemmons. I'm letting you both know right now that I have no hard feelings and I completely respect your decision.

Both men avoided eye contact and neither said a word.

"Honey," Pastor Gaines said, addressing his wife, Kendra, "After the meeting adjourns please contact Samantha and let her know that the fundraiser is a go. Tell her to print up the flyers and make sure she emphasizes that it will take place from 10am-2pm and that tickets can be purchased online or at the door. Also, please have her confirm that the Martin Brothers Gallery is still willing to donate a few photographs for us to auction off. We need to get the ball rolling and make sure Saturday is a huge success. We have exactly five days to make it happen."

"Yes, Pastor," Kendra said beaming.

"If all minds are clear, Deacon Clemmons, please close us out in prayer."

Deacon Clemmons nodded his head and cleared his throat. "Please bow your heads."

A few of the other board members rolled their eyes at the pastor's prayer selection. The deacon was longwinded and always prayed with his eyes wide open. He caught and stared into the eyes of anyone who made contact with him. His stare was intimidating, so everyone was sure to keep their eyes closed and heads bowed the entire time he prayed.

This afternoon's prayer was long, as usual, and although his words weren't exactly faith-filled, he poured out his heart to the Lord and ended by thanking God for his church family.

"In Jesus' name. Amen."

Ten voices echoed, "Amen."

After a few minutes of small talk, the board members made their way to the parking lot. Pastor Gaines and Kendra remained.

"I'm proud of you, honey," she said and rubbed her hand along the small of his back. He leaned in as she gently kissed him on his dimpled cheek.

"Thank you, baby. That means a lot. It's so hard to convince people that I have heard from God. They question *everything* I say. Even when they *agree* with me, they question what I say," he shook his head.

"I know. But you handled yourself well. And honestly, God didn't make you the leader for nothing. *You* are the visionary. And everyone else may not be able to see the vision you receive, but that's alright. They'll see the end-result and their faith will be increased because of it."

"True. It's obvious that none of them really believe this idea is going to work. But it will. It *has* to. I trust God to do what He showed me."

"Always." Kendra embraced her husband. He could feel the tension leave his body. Her encouragement relaxed him. Her presence was the personification of peace. Sweet peace.

"I'm going to give Samantha a call and then I'll meet you at the car," Kendra said and headed toward the conference room door.

"Thank you, sweetheart," he replied.

Alone, Pastor Gaines sat in the plush leather chair at the head of the maple conference table and focused his attention on a plaque that hung opposite his chair. *Now faith is the substance of things hoped for, the evidence of things not seen.* He had preached about faith more times than he could count. Making this fundraiser happen was a test of his faith... so far things were headed in the right direction.

He completely understood why the board didn't think this idea would work. The financial situation of the church did cast a dark cloud over the future of the ministry-but Pastor Gaines didn't doubt the vision that God had given him.

He had enough faith to move this mountain.

He looked to heaven and prayed for strength to match his faith.

***

The alarm clock sounded promptly at 6am. Pastor Gaines reached to turn it off and noticed the sunlight he was accustomed to at this time in the morning was missing in action. He also felt a nagging pain in his right arm. Whenever his joints stiffened rain was surely on the horizon. The weather forecast yesterday had been rain for Saturday, but it seemed so unlikely considering temperatures all the days leading up to Saturday were 75 degrees or higher.

"What's this about, Lord?" he asked aloud and grimaced as he grabbed the headboard to stretch out his arms.

The smell of Apple-wood smoked bacon permeated the bedroom and he knew that Kendra had prepared his favorite for this special day. When he walked into the living room he noticed that the news was on. The weatherman said the approaching storm would be the worst Long Beach had seen in a while. The rain was expected to start at 7am and not let up until at least 7pm. Pastor Gaines looked at Kendra. She attempted to seem undisturbed by the report and busied herself with breakfast.

"Did you hear that, hon?" he asked.

"Yes dear. But you know these weathermen are always wrong. It will probably be sunny all day."

Pastor Gaines walked to the window and pulled back the curtains. The sky was gray and the sound of thunder crackled in the background. Kendra's eyes widened.

"I think he got it right this time," he said and looked disappointedly at his wife.

"What do you want to do?" she asked as she took a glass out of the cabinet.

He shook his head. "I received specific instructions from God. The show must go on-rain or shine."

Pastor Gaines plopped down on the couch, hands over face. The fate of the church depended on this day. The bank would have to receive a full payment by Monday morning if they expected to keep their doors open for another month. Pastor Gaines thought back to the words of Deacon Blake. Maybe the focus of the church should have been growing the congregation instead of giving people the unadulterated truth of God's word. Then maybe none of these financial troubles would exist.

Pastor Gaines took a few deep breaths and reminded himself about the vision he had been shown. His doubt was quickly washed away by an unexplainable peace he often experienced when he set his anxieties to the side long enough to pray.

He thanked God, in advance, for the success of today's fundraiser and made his way to the table, where Kendra had set a plate of bacon, hashed browns, two poached eggs, two homemade biscuits, fried apples, a cup of coffee and a glass of orange juice. After she sat down with her own bowl of Old Fashioned Oats, they gave thanks and ate.

No sooner than Pastor Gaines finished his meal did the phone ring. He walked to the wall-mounted phone and answered it on the fourth ring.

It was Deacon Thorne asking if he had heard the weather report and if the event would still take place.

"Yes," Pastor Gaines responded. We can do everything inside the church. It will be fine."

He paused as he listened to Deacon Thorne's concerns and then said, "Yes, I heard that, but we can't let a little rain stop us." Then, after another pause, "I completely understand your position. I'm sorry you won't be able to make it out, but thanks for letting me know. He hung up the phone after saying goodbye.

He stared at Kendra for a moment. The disappointment in his eyes must have mirrored the disappointment in hers.

"I'm going to go take a shower," Pastor Gaines finally said.

***

Pastor Gaines wore a plaid button down shirt, a pair of dark blue jeans, black rain boots, and a black hooded rain coat. He put on a black beanie to protect his locks from the rain. When he walked back into the kitchen he noticed that Kendra had put on her rain coat and boots and was sitting at the kitchen table with a worried look on her face. Thunder shook the air around them.

"We received a few more cancellations while you were in the shower," she said.

Pastor Gaines was noticeably disturbed by this information. "Who?"

"The Anointed Messengers' agent said that their flight was cancelled and they won't be able to make it. Sis. Petunia said her sciatica is acting up today. And

Deacons Griffin, Hines, and Cody said they won't be able to make it."

Pastor Gaines sat down at the table, put his elbows on his knees and looked at the faux hardwood floor.

"What are you thinking, babe?" Kendra asked.

"I just don't understand what God is doing this time. I know what He told me to do, but none of this makes sense. It was 80 degrees yesterday." There's so much pressure riding on today and so far things aren't looking good. If I fail…"

Kendra interrupted. "There is no such thing as failure when you are obedient to God. I checked the website and about 50 people bought tickets online. $500. That's good news."

Pastor Gaines sighed. "Yes. That's great. But you know how California people are. It drizzles and they swear there's a flood and they can't leave the house. When it really does storm, they don't know what to do with themselves. I just wish I knew what God was doing. Rain. Today. Of all days."

"I wish I could do something," Kendra said and rubbed his shoulders.

***

There was a part of Pastor Gaines that wanted to cancel the event once he actually got behind the wheel and saw the fury of the storm. The streets were near-empty. There were flash floods on almost every corner and the winds seemed tornado-fierce. The staff that was supposed to help set up had all called or texted to back out. But out of obedience, Pastor Gaines and Kendra pressed on and made it to church shortly before 8am.

They worked tirelessly to get everything ready. Kendra set out the sandwiches, chips, and bottled water she had dropped off at the church the afternoon before. Then she set up tables for the silent auction and raffle. Pastor Gaines hung banners and balloons throughout the fellowship hall and then looked over his notecards where he had written words of encouragement to speak towards the end of the fundraiser. Kendra organized guest welcome cards and bibles for those interested in remaining in fellowship with the church. Once everything looked just right, Kendra sat down at the piano and played a few chords to keep herself occupied while they waited for their first guest.

At ten o'clock, the church doors were unlocked. They remained closed to keep the rain out. Laminated signs announcing the fundraiser and a couple of balloons were taped on the outside doors, however shortly after Pastor Gaines put them up, the rain and wind whisked them away.

Outside thunder roared as lightening lit the sky simultaneously. Pastor Gaines and Kendra could see through the windows that the lightening was dangerously close. But instead of despairing, they worshipped God in the fellowship hall alone until 2pm. They prayed and sang praises to God. They listened to Tye Tribbett on Kendra's iPod, which she had connected to the surround sound system, and they danced like David danced. They worshipped God with every bit of their being in the midst of the storm until finally the time had come to close up shop.

Just as they started to pack things up, Pastor Gaines noticed a beam of sunlight shining through the windows. He walked to the door and opened it.

"Kendra, do you see this?"

The rain had completely stopped.

"You have got to be kidding me," she said as she looked out the door. She shook her head in disbelief.

"I just don't understand," Pastor Gaines said with a twinge of frustration in his voice. He closed the door and sat down in a folding chair next to where Kendra stood.

"It happened this way for a reason. God must have something up His sleeve," she said and placed a hand on his shoulder.

Pastor Gaines didn't respond.

"I'm proud of you, honey," Kendra said.

"Thanks. That means a lot," he said as he looked at her and smiled.

"Well," Kendra said, "let's finish getting this place cleaned up so we can get home. I want to whip you in a game of Dominos."

"Kendra you already know that will NEVER happen," he said. He stood up and kissed her on the cheek. They both laughed and continued cleaning.

At 2:45pm, Pastor Gaines and Kendra were in his office putting away the last of the event decorations when he noticed an envelope on his desk. On top of it was a Post-it that said, "I didn't open this because it said

CONFIDENTIAL. I hope everything goes well with the fundraiser. You know I'd be there if I could. God Bless, Samantha."

Pastor Gaines looked at the Priority envelope but didn't recognize the sender's name. He sat down and opened it.

"What's that?" Kendra asked.

"I'm not sure."

He pulled out a letter and read it aloud:

Dear Pastor Gaines,

My wife and I watch your webcast every Sunday and have been so inspired by your sincerity and the way you present the word of God. My wife and I live in Dallas and although we won't be able to attend the fundraiser, we want to be a part of the great things God is doing through you.

My son, Manny, battled with addiction and depression for many years. He was in St. John's Drug & Psychiatric Treatment Center, where he told me he met you. He said you prayed with him and introduced him to the Lord. You helped him through a very difficult time. He passed away a few months ago, but because of the time he spent with you, my wife and I are confident that he went home to be with our Lord. Although there is no amount we could give to say thank you for allowing the love of God to emanate through you and taking time out to minister to someone so many others had overlooked, we hope this small token of appreciation will help you reach your financial goals for the church.

We pray that God continue to bless you and your entire church family and we hope to visit you soon.

With Love,

Ed and Judy Ricketts

P.S. Manny's birthday was also April 5th. He would have been 30 years old this year.

"I remember you telling me about Manny," Kendra said.

"Yeah. He's the one that gave His life to Christ my very first year at the center. I'm ashamed to say I haven't talked to him in about a year. When he moved back to Texas, we kinda just lost touch," Pastor Gaines said ashamedly as he wiped a tear from his eye. "I hadn't even heard about his passing. I wonder if anyone from the center knows he died. Three months ago? I feel horrible."

"Oh, babe," Kendra said and rubbed his shoulder, "Don't be so hard on yourself. Everything happens for a reason. And Manny knew that you loved him. And from the note it sounds like he was still following Christ when he died."

"Yeah. I'm glad he reconnected with his parents before he died because when I first met him he was embarrassed about his addiction and had really shut them out of his life. But God always has a plan," Pastor Gaines said.

"Yes, He does," Kendra agreed.

Pastor Gaines wiped another tear from his eye and sighed.

A smaller envelope was sealed and enclosed within the larger one. Pastor Gaines opened it and pulled out a check. When he saw the amount he was shocked. It was the largest check he had ever seen. He blinked to be sure he was seeing correctly. Then he handed the check to Kendra.

"Oh my God!" she shrieked and fell to her knees. "Praise God!"

***

The congregation anxiously awaited Pastor Gaines' big announcement. Everyone knew about the failure of the previous days' event and had known about the church's financial woes for some time. They figured Pastor Gaines would be announcing their eviction or some other bad news at the service. Worship service started out dry.

When it was time for the message, Pastor Gaines stood on the dais and prayed. The sullen congregation occasionally chimed in with moans and "Yes Lord's." When the prayer was over, Pastor Gaines said, "Israel Christian Fellowship. As you know God placed it on my heart a little over a month ago to hold a fundraising event yesterday. And as you all know, the weather was some of the worst in our history. Sis. Gaines and I were the only ones here, but in obedience we set up and worshipped God anyhow. Our guest performers cancelled and not one person came out to support. Not one person."

"Well…" a few members sang from the audience.

"Sis. Gaines and I had every reason in the world to feel defeated. Things didn't look good at all. I didn't understand how this could happen when I heard so clearly from the Lord that this was something *He* wanted us to do on the 5th day of April. The trustees and deacons will tell you that they all thought I was crazy for investing what little we had in our bank account to make the day happen. And the rain confirmed that."

"Well…" more than a couple members agreed. A few of the deacons shifted in their seats. Deacon Clemmons wiped his head with a gray handkerchief. Deacon Blake bit into a peppermint and rocked back and forth the way he always did right before saying, "I told you so." Church fans waved vigorously as the congregation listened for the inevitable bad news.

"And would you believe that the rain completely stopped shortly after two? Just like that." His voice rose excitedly as he re-emphasized, "The sun broke through the clouds *just like that*. The rain lasted *just* long enough to ruin the fundraiser…just long enough to make many wonder whether I had actually heard from God…just long enough to have the first lady and me sitting there trying to figure out what God was up to. But let me tell you about the God I serve.

"I went into my office, and on my desk was a letter from the parents of a young man I counseled at St. John's Treatment Center. I've never met his parents, but they wrote a letter of appreciation for the kindness I showed to their son, Manny, who battled addiction and depression for many years and recently passed away. They said they follow our services online, heard about the fundraiser, and wanted to do something special to honor Manny. His birthday also happened to be April 5th. He would have been thirty years old yesterday. And I am so happy to tell you all today just how *good* God is. The drought is over, church. God moved through Manny's parents, and they sent Israel Christian Fellowship a check for.........three hundred thousand dollars."

Gasps were heard all over the sanctuary.

Sis. Petunia jumped out of her seat and hollered, "Thank you, Jesus!"

Deacon Blake's and Deacon Clemmons' mouths dropped. Within seconds they were on their feet clapping as well.

The organist laid on a chord and held it before breaking into a gospel run. His fingers danced quickly across the keys and his foot pushed on the expression pedal. The congregation clapped to the beat.

"You see, there are no coincidences with God. He's always up to something good, even when it seems like

He's not thinking about us," Pastor Gaines said through the excitement. "I feel like shouting, church."

"Yeah," the congregation enthusiastically agreed.

"I said, I feel like shouting church!"

"Yeah," they replied.

"God is so faithful. I didn't understand His plan, but I obeyed His command to the letter and He was faithful to do just what He said He would do…exceeding abundantly above all I could ever ask or think."

"Hallelujah!"

Pastor Gaines caught the eyes of Kendra. She was out of her seat with her white handkerchief flying back and forth smiling proudly at her husband. He smiled at her and mouthed a thank you. Kendra nodded. Then Pastor Gaines raised his hands and eyes toward Heaven and thanked God.

Diagnosis

"I will always be by your side. And I will pray for you each day. Comfort you through all the pain, gently kiss your fears away, you can turn to me and cry, always understand that I give you all I have inside..."

-Unknown

"Mrs. Watson, I'm going to give you a list of three words and I want you to repeat them to me," the doctor said. "Penny, table, apple."

My mom's eyes shifted from side to side as she tried to recall the words.

"Uh. Penny. Let's see. Penny."

"Penny, table, and apple. Can you remember those words?"

"Penny. Uh. Penny. Table. I - I don't know."

"Ok Mrs. Watson, I would like you to add these numbers in your head. What is 73 plus 29?"

"Let's see. I could do it if I had my paper and pen. Let's see. Three plus nine is - 12. Carry the one. Um. I - I could do it with a paper and pen, but just off the top of my head - let's see."

"Mrs. Watson, please draw these shapes for me - Square. Circle. Triangle."

With her inability to respond correctly to each request, things she could have easily done two years ago, I watched her become more and more frustrated. She stood up and informed everyone that she was leaving. She said that she refused to sit in front of these White doctors and have them disrespect her by insinuating she was ignorant.

"I have a college degree," she informed them. "I went to Livingstone College and majored in Business Education. I taught at El Monte High for many years," she said indignantly as she searched for her purse and other belongings.

"Mom, please calm down," I said and rushed to her side. "Please just have a seat. No one thinks you're stupid. We're just trying to figure out what's going on and make sure you get the help you need. Please, mom."

"You really think this will help?" she asked, her 73-year old eyes looking to me for the truth.

"Yes, I do," I said. *God, I sure hope it does.*

"OK."

She sat down.

The questions continued.

"Mrs. Watson, who is the president of the United States? Who was the president before him? And the one before him? Who was his wife? How many years did you teach at El Monte? How many brothers and sisters do you have? How many children? Grandchildren? What are their names? How old are they? When is your birthday? What is your address? Where were you born? What is your favorite television show? What is your favorite color? How old are you? Tell me about your husband. How long have you been married? How old are your children? What kind of cancer did you have? How long did you receive treatment? Do you ever feel sad? Do you feel like your life has purpose?"

Question after question she gave answers that she was obviously unsure of.

First there was the geriatric specialist. Then the neurologist. Psychiatrist. Social worker. Questions. X-Rays. MRIs. Physical exams. 8 hours. Mom hung in there, as frustrating as I'm sure it was for her.

We told them about the delirium she had been experiencing lately - about the two-headed man who was trying to hurt my family, about my dad's adopted cat that she absolutely loathed and felt he kept to spite her, about the burning flesh in the woods, about her running to neighbors' houses in the middle of the night because "something's going on," about her newfound distrust of those she formerly trusted the most, about her recent trip to North Carolina, and her experience at the facility for people with memory loss.

She even told them about the time her jaw was broken and about being struck by lightning as a child.

I was proud of her bravery and honesty.

At the end of 8 hours, the diagnosis was made. Alzheimer's. Quite likely its effects were sped up by the recent cancer treatments she had received. The disease was degenerative. There was no cure. Recommendations for medications were made. They encouraged her to do puzzles, read magazine articles, try to recall what they were about, and do other activities to help her stay as sharp as possible for as long as possible. If she remained healthy, she could live for many years, but she would continue to get worse. She would eventually forget the names of her children. As time passed, she wouldn't be able to shower or get dressed by herself. It was also certain that she would have to wear diapers and be changed each day. Incontinence was the word they used.

If cancer should show up anywhere in her body, they advised against future chemo or radiation treatments. Based on her history, they didn't see the purpose. It would likely cause more harm than good. Their recommendation was to try our hardest to enjoy each day that we are blessed to see and make her as comfortable as possible.

Before the geriatric specialist finished talking I broke down. My plan to be strong for her flew right out the window as the doctor confirmed what I already knew in my heart. I guess it made it more real to hear him say it.

The social worker took me to another room and allowed me to cry and talk. She reminded me that doctors don't have the final say. God is in control.

In the car on the way home my mother was obviously upset. She didn't like any of what they said. She told me not to cry because they didn't know what they were talking about. They had wasted her time.

What was also obvious was that she didn't even remember the diagnosis they had given. All she knew was that she was hungry and her arm hurt. She also knew that she didn't want me to tell anyone what the doctors had said - not even my dad. I told her that was one wish I couldn't honor. He needed to know. And so did my brother and sister. It was nothing to be ashamed of and we would all do our best to love her through it.

Holiday Party

"I appreciate honesty more than anything. If you tell me what it is up front, you give me the option to take it or leave it. I respect that."

-Unknown

"Did I tell you how amazing you look tonight?" Greg asked as our car approached the valet stand positioned under a street lamp directly in front of Rhonda's massive home.

I blushed and smiled at my handsome husband. Even after a year of dating and five years of marriage, his smooth voice, dark chocolate skin, and deep dimples still gave me butterflies.

"Yes, but you can tell me again," I said, batting my faux lashes.

Greg grinned naughtily and looked me in my eyes. I melted, as usual.

"Kelly, you are the most beautiful woman I have ever laid eyes on." He kissed me on my ear and rubbed my belly.

"Thank you, baby," I said as I placed my clutch in my lap.

My window was rolled down just a little and I could hear Snoop's "Santa Claus Goes Straight to the Ghetto" blaring from Rhonda's house. The number of cars that lined the street and the bodies I could see moving to the beat through her front window let me know that the party was already in full swing.

The valet pulled on my door handle and helped me out of our silver Volkswagen Passat. Greg rushed around to my side and gently held my hand as we walked toward Rhonda's front door. There wasn't a trace of fog, which was unusual considering the time of year and our proximity to LAX.

I was six months pregnant and my body still wasn't used to the extra weight. Standing, sitting, walking, laying, and just about everything else was extremely uncomfortable. I tried to make it look easy and even though I had found a cute pair of ballerina shoes to match my outfit, I'm sure I looked as awkward as I felt.

"You look fine," Greg assured me, as if he could tell what I was thinking.

"Thanks," I said and smoothed my "little black dress." I had worn it many times before my pregnancy and was happy that the flared waist allowed me to fit it easily even now.

Rhonda opened her front door before we rang the bell. She was fabulous, as always. Her jet-black hair was parted down the center and lay perfectly mid-stomach. She wore a tight red A-line dress with a black belt and three-inch black heels. She had on a Santa hat with her name stitched across the front. Bright red lipstick accentuated her pouty lips and her gold accessories brought the look together.

Rhonda and Greg had been friends since childhood. He introduced me to her shortly after we started dating, and although the two of us hadn't grown to be the best of friends, we did talk occasionally and hung out in party settings at least twice a year. I admired her style. She was confident, connected, and well respected. She had an easy way of making you feel like royalty whenever you were in her presence. I liked that.

"My two favorite people," she said as she pulled Greg and me in for a group hug that lasted a little too long. Her slurred words highlighted the spirits on her breath. Her glassy dark-brown eyes were a sure sign of an interesting night.

"Thank you for having us," Greg said and kissed her on the cheek.

"I'll take your coats," she said and sloppily hung them in the entry closet.

I glanced around the room. Rhonda was quite the party planner. From the decorations and the h'ors deurves to the music and the guests, Rhonda never disappointed. She had cleared her great room and dining room of most of their furniture, creating one huge dance floor that extended through the French doors and onto her patio. The space smelled of fresh pine, and red, white, and silver decorations were sprinkled throughout. It was breathtaking. There were already about 50 guests present and every one of them, with the exception of us, was dancing.

"Let's dance, babe," Greg said as he pulled me onto the dance floor.

"Enjoy," I heard Rhonda call after us.

The DJ played Mariah's "All I Want for Christmas is You" and Greg and I proceeded to do what we did best.

I always liked to see who would be at Rhonda's gatherings. Her travels and career as a film producer kept her in touch with some rather entertaining people. She had a way of mixing A-list Hollywood types with middle school administrators like Greg and me. No one ever seemed uncomfortable and egos never seemed to be an issue. Her parties promised good times and laughs for all.

This year, reality star Milo Briggs was rubbing elbows with Christian Whitaker, supporting actor in the highest grossing Black movie of all time. Christian obviously had no interest in what Milo was talking about, but he nodded and eyed the hostess who was overtly flirting behind Milo's back.

Shawn Hines, BET News Anchor, had his eye on the same pretty little waitress that Christian was eyeing. I leaned over and asked Greg who he thought would woo the girl. Greg gave it to Christian hands down.

"The news is too boring for someone like her," Greg teased.

We both laughed, but of course I had to speak up for her. She looked like a smart young lady who would rather be a main squeeze than just one of many. For that reason, I believed she would choose brains over beauty.

As we danced, we occasionally leaned in to share scoop about the party goers around us. I noticed Rhonda gazing in our direction a couple times. I put both thumbs up and smiled to let her know we were having a good time. As soon as the disc jockey played "This Christmas," Greg looked over my shoulder and his face lit up with excitement.

"Aw, babe, look. I see my boy, Theo. I haven't seen him in a minute."

I turned and spotted Theo, a head above everyone else. He smiled as he walked in our direction. Although I had never actually met him in person, he looked exactly the same as he did on all the pictures of him that Greg had shown me.

Greg had told me on many occasions how Theo had taken him under his wing and treated him like family when he was a freshman at Howard. Theo joined the Marines immediately after he graduated and although he and Greg still emailed one another, they hadn't actually seen each other since college.

I stepped to the side as they greeted each other with a handshake that ended with the "Kid 'n Play." I couldn't help but laugh.

"Greg, my man! Long time!"

"Yeah, man. I see you finally decided to just cut it all off," Greg teased.

"What can I say? The ladies love a bald head."

They laughed and then his buddy glanced in my direction and said, "Who is this pretty lady and what is she doing with you?"

I blushed.

"Back, back!" Greg joked. "This is my wife, Kelly. Kelly, this is my boy Theo."

"I've heard a lot about you, Theo. It's nice to *finally* put a face with the name."

He extended his hand and politely said, "It's a pleasure to meet you. And don't believe *anything* you've heard. I was a kid back then."

"I've only heard good things," I smiled, returning his positive vibes.

While Greg and Theo caught up, I excused myself and perused the room. I noticed that the hostess was cozying up to Christian, who appeared confident she would leave with him tonight. Greg had been right.

"Hey, Kelly," I heard Rhonda's voice over my shoulder as she approached me.

I turned and smiled.

"Girl, you look like you are having way too much fun," I said with a chuckle.

"Not at all," she said seriously. "Can we talk?" Her words were more garbled than they had been when we first arrived. It hadn't even been an hour.

"Sure," I said.

"Come on."

She grabbed my hand and escorted me to the patio. There were tents and plush seating set up along the perimeter of the yard. The pool on the far side was lit with red lights. The palmettos and shrubbery that lined her backyard were decorated with red and white Christmas bulbs. Rhonda and I walked past dancing guests to the tent at the end of the yard and we sat down.

"You've done it again!" I smiled. "Great party."

Her eyes were glassy and I could tell that she hadn't heard a word I said.

"You look pretty," she said with a loud sigh.

"Thank you. I feel like a whale," I said quite frankly and laughed.

"No. You look beautiful," she slurred and shook her head.

"Thank you."

"I'm jealous."

"No way!" I laughed. There was absolutely no way she was jealous of me on my best day, and especially not with the watermelon I was carrying around in my stomach. "You know I look like a cow."

"Not at all," she said as she broke down and sobbed.

I didn't quite know what to do, so I rubbed her back and then pulled her into a quick tight embrace.

"What's wrong?"

She didn't respond. I couldn't imagine what was so horrible that it was worth her messing up her gorgeous face at *her* own party. Whatever it was, I just hoped I'd be able to console her.

The disc jockey mixed in Run DMC's "Christmas in Hollis" and a wave of energy erupted on the dance floor. Guests hollered, "Oh snap," and hands flew in the air as heads bobbed to the beat. This was my song and as difficult as it was, I kept the largest part of my attention on Rhonda.

"It shoulda been me," she finally said.

I rubbed her shoulder. I didn't quite know what she was referring to, but I was happy that she felt comfortable enough with me to cry in front of me. This was a first.

"With Greg," she continued.

I held my breath and waited for her to finish her sentence. It took me a few seconds to realize that she already had.

"What do you mean?" I asked.

"Did Greg ever tell you that I was supposed to have his baby?" she asked.

No. I hadn't heard that at all. I dropped my hand onto my lap.

"What do you mean?" I asked again, my mind racing.

"Greg and I dated in college. He even proposed to me, but I said no. I should be the one he's married to. I should be the one having his child."

"Let me get this straight. You and Greg-"

"Yes," she cut me off.

"But he told me that you guys have always been *just* friends."

She didn't respond.

I didn't know what to say or do. I felt betrayed. I was quite positive all the emotions I felt were visible at that very moment.

I didn't say another word. I left her sitting there and headed to the restroom to splash water on my face.

I felt my body temperature rise and I fanned back tears with my hand. I couldn't believe what she'd just said.

I thought back to the time I'd asked Greg if they'd ever dated.

"No," he'd said.

"Why not? She's gorgeous."

"She's not my type," he had replied firmly.

That had been hard to believe. I mean, Rhonda had to have been one of *the* most attractive women *I* had ever met. She had dark chocolate skin and the most entrancing dark brown eyes. I could only wish for a body as well-proportioned as hers.

I had pressed Greg to explain why she wasn't his type. He assured me that he was a man of substance and there were things about Rhonda I didn't know. He swore that although he cared about her as a friend, it stopped there.

He'd said just what I wanted to hear. I didn't want to breathe life in a place where Greg assured me there'd been none and so I left it alone.

Now here I was, in the bathroom, confused, hurt, and upset. What else had Greg lied about? If he couldn't be honest about his past relationship with Rhonda, could I believe that he had been honest about anything else? I wanted to scream. I had to talk with Greg to see whether there was any truth to the story.

I opened the bathroom door and headed in the direction where I had left Theo and Greg. I could feel the baby kicking as I walked and I rubbed my stomach to soothe her.

"I need to talk to you," I said as I approached and interrupted Greg, who was still engrossed in conversation with Theo.

He turned and looked at me-his face an amalgam of shock, confusion, and concern.

"Is everything alright? Have you been crying?" Greg asked as he stood and gently held my shoulders. He attempted to kiss me on the forehead, but I stepped back before he could. From the corner of my eye I could see Theo pull out his cell phone and *pretend* to answer a text message.

"Let's get out of here," I said.

"Alright if you insist," he said and turned to tell Theo he would catch up with him later.

"Let me say bye to Rhonda," he said to me.

"Let's just go," I said resolutely.

Greg looked taken aback. I could tell by the rapid movement of his eyes that he was searching my face for understanding.

"Alright. After you," Greg finally said.

I marched toward the front door and grabbed my coat from the closet.

The cold air hit and chilled my face as soon as I stepped outside. A layer of fog was nestled at our shins.

Greg handed the valet the ticket for our car and when he ran off to fetch it, Greg reached for my hand and said, "Babe, I sure wish you would tell me what's got you so upset."

"You lied to me, Greg. I can't believe you would lie to me."

"What are you talking about?"

"What do you think I'm talking about? What all have you lied to me about?"

I stared him in his guilty eyes-eyes that had always seemed so authentic to me. I was disgusted.

"I have always been completely honest with you."

"The fact that you are lying to me right now pisses me off even more, Greg."

Greg lifted his hand. "Baby, look, I think your hormones…"

"Don't touch me. And don't you dare blame my hormones for me being upset because you lied about you and Rhonda."

Greg's whole demeanor changed. He shifted nervously.

"It's not what you think," he said.

"Well explain to me what it is because in my estimation, you blatantly lied. I asked you whether the two of you dated…and you *never* mentioned that she once carried your child."

"I'm not sure what she told you, but it wasn't like that. And she NEVER carried my child."

"I can't stand anymore lies, so unless you plan to be completely honest with me, I don't even want to hear it."

The valet pulled up and ran around to open my door. I angrily got in and slammed my door before he could close it for me. Greg handed him a few dollars and thanked him before getting in and pulling off.

Greg made a few turns before we ended up at the scenic overlook in Culver City. This had been one of our favorite places to sit and talk since our dating days. He drove up the winding road in silence and parked the car.

The skies that were so clear earlier in the night were now occupied by a thick layer of fog. The fog made the view seem non-existent.

Greg cracked the windows, turned off the motor, and faced me. I had never seen his face so full of dread.

"Look. Rhonda and I dated for a week when we were freshmen in college. It was actually less than a week."

"You told me that you were just friends-that you had never been romantic."

"We have *never* been romantic," he said.

I rolled my eyes and faced the window. "But the two of you were in a relationship? I can't imagine you not being romantic with her," I said.

"Yes. We were friends and we thought we'd give a relationship a shot, but we decided we were much better as friends. It took us less than a week to realize that."

"Did you guys kiss during this 'week'?"

He paused for a moment, his face a ball of loathing. "Yes," he said, "But never before or after those few days we were in a relationship."

"So did you get her pregnant?"

"No. I hadn't ever been with anyone in that way. Right after we started talking Rhonda told me she was pregnant. When she told me I was the father, I knew it was impossible since we had never been together, and I also knew that although I loved her like a friend, there was no way I could be in a serious relationship with her."

"Where's the baby?"

"Kelly, I don't know if she ever *was* pregnant," he said and shook his head. "I never saw a baby. And we never talked about it," Greg said.

"She said you proposed to her."

"Not true," he answered firmly.

"Why did you keep her around as a friend after she lied to you? I just don't understand that."

Greg took a deep breath and looked at me with sad eyes. "The thing I never told you about Rhonda is that she had a very rough upbringing. You know I lived right next door to her and we talked about everything growing up. She told me that her mother hated her and her stepfather beat the crap out of her every day. You should've seen some of the bruises he left on her. It was horrible. I felt bad for her. And I guess knowing what she had been through made it hard for me to turn my back on her. Before we tried the whole relationship thing we were friends-best friends. I didn't want to let go of our friendship."

I felt a lump in my throat and breathing became difficult. I turned the key in the ignition and rolled my window down a little more.

"Why didn't you ever tell me any of this?" I asked as I turned the car back off.

"Kelly, I don't know," he sighed. Most people are dishonest about *something* when they first start talking to someone."

"I was completely honest with you about *everything*," I reminded him as I cut my eyes in his direction.

"You're right. Look. I'm sorry. I never meant to hurt you. I was only trying to protect you. You had nothing to worry about with Rhonda. She was really just my *friend*. I guess I thought if I told you about our less than a week relationship when we first started talking, you might want me to end my friendship with her."

"You're absolutely right about that," I said, and rolled my eyes. "I feel so stupid. Everybody told me that I was a fool for thinking the two of you had never been together, but I just knew you would never lie to me."

"I wanted to tell you, but it got harder as time passed. I'm sorry, babe," he said and reached for my hand.

I pulled it away.

"Do you know how many "friends" I gave up for you, Greg? All of them," I reminded him. "You were worth it to me."

Neither of us spoke for a while. I looked out my window and wiped away an occasional tear.

Just then, his cell phone went off. He sent the call to voicemail. My cell phone rang next. I pulled it out of my clutch and saw Rhonda's face on the screen. I sent her to voicemail. My phone rang again. I turned the ringer off and put it back in my purse. Greg's phone rang next. He sent the call to voicemail and turned his ringer off as well. I glanced in his direction, rolled my eyes, and then looked back out the window.

"Look, Kelly. I'm sorry I lied to you. That was selfish of me. It was wrong," he said.

I kept my gaze out my window.

"I will do whatever it takes to make it up to you."

I responded with silence.

What could he do to make this up to me? For start, Rhonda would have to be taken out of our equation. That was for sure. I liked her, but I couldn't imagine being in her presence after tonight. She was intoxicated at the party, yes, but I believe people say exactly what they mean when they are. Then when they sober up they feel remorseful and try to convince the people they hurt while intoxicated that they didn't mean anything they said. She meant to hurt me and she was in love with my husband. Two things that meant she had to go permanently.

"So here's what has to happen," I finally said. "First of all, you already know that you maintaining a friendship with Rhonda after tonight is out of the question. We will both talk with her tomorrow and make that clear."

He nodded and said, "Alright."

"That easy?"

"Yes, baby. You are worth more to me than anything and anyone else in this world," he said. His eyes pleaded for me to believe him.

I looked down at my hands and continued. "Second, I need you to reassure me that I can trust you and I don't know how you can do that. I know it's going to take some time though because right now I'm feeling like the whole six years we've been together has been built on a foundation of your dishonesty."

"Baby, that hurts. I haven't lied about anything else."

"That sounds good, Greg," I said and looked up to make eye contact, "but yesterday morning you would have told me you had never lied to me about anything at all only for tonight to happen."

Greg dropped his head.

"The third thing that's going to have to happen from this moment on is that you never make a decision to 'protect' me that involves withholding information or flat out lying to me. I'm a big girl, Greg. I can handle it."

Greg looked up and arrested my eyes with his. He reached for my hand. This time, I didn't pull away.

"I'm so sorry, Kelly. I love you more than anything in this world and I promise I will *never* be dishonest with you again."

I exhaled for the first time in a long time. I absolutely believed him.

The space around us felt completely different than it had ever felt before. It felt-pure. I was happy to know the complete truth about Greg's relationship with Rhonda-the truth that I myself had chosen to overlook for so long.

In a sense, I was just as much to blame for lying to myself as he was for lying to me. I loved Greg enough to ignore the tug in my heart that let me know there was more to his story with Rhonda six years ago when I first felt it. I loved him so much that whenever thoughts about his possible past with Rhonda ran across my mind, I ignored them too. And if I was completely honest, there was nothing else that he had ever told me that sat as uneasily with me as his "friendship" with Rhonda. Greg was a good man. And I loved him.

"You'd better not," I said finally answering him, and I leaned my head against the headrest.

I closed my eyes and exhaled again. It felt so good to breathe in an atmosphere of truth. Of course I still felt the residual effects of the emotional rollercoaster I'd been on tonight, but now it was time to open myself to the freedom that forgiveness and healing brings. And the love that Greg and I shared was completely worth it all.

Barb and Mildred

"Giving our children everything they want makes them demanding and ungrateful. And they never learn how to be self-controlled. Think about this next time you give in to your screaming child."

-Unknown

Barb and her daughter Mildred were both senior citizens. But in Barb's eyes Mildred still acted like a teenager. Two failed marriages, three misfit children, one ulcer, and one weight loss surgery later, and Mildred continued to make what Barb considered poor decisions. But Mildred was her only living child-and Barb loved her.

At eighty-seven, Barb had amazing genes. If it weren't for her head full of grays, she might even look younger than Mildred, who had just turned seventy. But Barb didn't believe in dying her hair.

Barb gently blew the cup of steaming hot coffee that she held in her hands. Her deep red lips pursed as if she were blowing kisses at the steam. The hazelnut aroma held her nostrils captive in sweet savoring goodness. Barb took a sip and set her cup down long enough to scowl at Mildred's choice of breakfast.

"I was trying not to say anything, but-pork bacon, dear? You must be *trying* to kill yourself," Barb said. Each word she spoke sounded as if she were singing second soprano in an off-off-Broadway musical.

"Oh mom! Not again. I deserve to treat myself once in a while," Mildred whined in her deep smoky voice as she rolled her eyes.

"That's not true, Mildee. You treated yourself most of your life and that's how you ended up the size of a small bus. There was no point in having that surgery ten years ago if you're just gonna pile the pounds back on."

"I know, mother. I'm watching what I eat."

"You watch it and then you eat it," Barb mumbled and cleared her throat.

Mildred rolled her eyes and took a bite of her thick-cut bacon.

"Look. I love you. I just don't want to have to bury another one of my children. I pray you never know how that feels," Barb said attempting to pull at Mildred's heart-strings. She forgot momentarily about Mildred's strained relationship with her children.

"Don't worry about me," Mildred said defensively as she scooped smothered potatoes drenched in ketchup into her mouth.

Barb shook her head and tried one final tactic.

"Sweetheart, oatmeal is a better option for you. Your father and I eat it seven days a week. Why do you think we're still so spry?"

Mildred sucked her teeth. "How do you know it isn't the Castor-oil? Or the mustard? Or the turmeric? Or the fruit and veggie smoothies? Or the fresh salads? Or any of the other 'healthy' things you do because you're so *perfect*?" she asked sarcastically.

Barb held up her hands in surrender.

"Oh I'm far from perfect," Barb said, trying to sound more modest than she actually was, "but you're right, dear. It could be any of those thing. The point is that we are taking great care of our bodies. You only get one, ya know."

Mildred rolled her eyes. "I would die from boredom if I put that stuff in my body *every* day."

Barb stirred her oatmeal, which she adorned with fresh blueberries and thought that after all these years,

Mildred was still intent on doing the exact opposite of everything she suggested. Sixty years ago when Barb complained about Mildred's stubbornness, people had said that she'd eventually grow out of it and start listening. Those people were wrong.

Barb took a bite of oatmeal and looked at Mildred intensely before changing the subject.

"So, how are the children?"

"Bill calls collect every day. I've started calling him 'Bill Collector,'" she said and laughed at her own wit. Her laugh was a loud snort followed by what sounded like gasps for air. Barb glanced around and smiled nervously at the patrons who were staring disgustedly at Mildred.

"I told him he should write letters instead of calling, but he says his arthritis acts up too bad for him to write," Mildred continued.

"You should send him some turmeric," offered Barb.

Mildred took a bite of bacon and didn't respond.

"And the girls?" Barb asked.

"I haven't talked with them," Mildred answered sharply.

Barb shook her head disappointedly. "Well I still pray for them every day. The last time I talked to Edith I told her that she should call you," Barb said as she took another sip of coffee.

Mildred didn't respond.

"How's the meal, ladies?" the waiter asked as he approached. Barb looked up at him and smiled. She loved well groomed waiters. This one looked like an actor. He wore a crisp white shirt with a black tie and black slacks. His jet black hair was spiked and gelled stiff.

"Delicious," Barb replied with a wink. She took a quick glance at his nametag. "Thanks for asking, Jason."

"Let me know if you ladies need anything else," he blushed.

"If you date older women, I have a friend who would be perfect for you. Her name's Shirley. She's 75, but she's young at heart," Barb said.

Jason smiled coyly and replied, "That's flattering, ma'am, but I'm married."

Barb looked at his left hand but didn't see a ring.

Seeming to notice, Jason shifted nervously and said, "I lost my ring a few days ago."

"That's not a good sign," Barb said and shook her head.

Jason seemed uncomfortable.

"I'd like a cola," Mildred interrupted.

"Coming right up," the waiter said, and quickly walked away.

"Soda for breakfast! Mildee."

"Mom, please!" Mildred couldn't hide her annoyance. "Just be happy I didn't order a cocktail. That's what I really want."

"Believe me I am. I just wish you'd at least ordered a diet cola."

"Diet doesn't taste the same."

Barb took a long sip of coffee. There was no sense trying to reason with Mildred, so she changed the subject.

"Can you believe that young fellow lost his ring? 71 years of marriage and your father and I never once misplaced our rings."

"He seems like a nice kid," Mildred said and continued eating.

"He may be nice but that doesn't change the fact that he is irresponsible," Barb said.

Mildred didn't respond.

Barb took a bite of oatmeal before easing into her next topic. "So, your father and I took a water aerobics class last week. It was good exercise. Something different, ya know? Your father's pretty good at it too."

"That's nice," Mildred said, seeming to know where the conversation was headed.

"I was thinking maybe you could go with us one day. It would be fun."

"Mom, I'm not tagging along with you and dad anymore. I'm seventy years old. I'm too old for that."

"That's ridiculous! You're never too old to spend time with your parents. I *wish* I could have spent time with my parents when I was your age," Barb said hoping to make Mildred feel a little guilty.

Mildred didn't appear to budge. She took a gulp of water and met her mother's stare.

"I saw some handsome guys your age there too. You might meet your next husband," Barb offered with a smile.

Mildred rolled her eyes. "Mom, look. I might as well just get to the point. The reason I invited you to take me out for breakfast is because I was wondering if I could borrow a couple dollars."

"What?" Barb was used to Mildred petitioning her for cash and figured that was the purpose of this meeting, but she was always a little taken aback when Mildred actually asked. "I thought we were working on our mother-daughter intimacy."

Mildred sucked her teeth and said, "I'm just a little short on my rent money and need to borrow a couple dollars."

Barb ate a few spoonfuls of oatmeal and took a sip of coffee while she gathered her thoughts. Mildred had overspent *again*. She was sure it was her latest trip to the casino that caused Mildred to be short again this month.

"We helped you last month, Mildee," Barb finally said.

"I know, but something else came up."

"What?"

"I really don't want to talk about it."

"Doesn't your social security and retirement cover rent and living expenses?"

"Yes, but I still have to eat and put gas in my car."

"You could stand to eat and drive a little less, don't you think?" Barb asked.

Mildred sucked her teeth again.

"What about your savings, dear? Is that gone too?"

"Mom I really don't want to talk about it. I wish I didn't have to ask you for money. But I really need help."

"Just tell me. Did you overspend at the casino?"

Mildred didn't answer.

Barb took a sip of coffee and looked Mildred in her eyes. She placed her hand on Mildred's hand and said very carefully, "Maybe you could move back in with-"

"Absolutely not!" Mildred protested and snatched her hand away. "There's no way in hell."

"Watch your language, young lady."

Mildred looked at her glass of water and said, "I apologize." She looked up and met Barb's hurt eyes and added, "Thanks for the offer but I am too old to live with my parents."

The waiter returned with the cola and sensing the tension quickly placed it in front of Mildred and scurried off.

Barb took a bite of wheat toast.

"Don't you think Jason would make a good model or actor?" Barb asked, hoping to lighten the mood.

"Sure. He'd probably be a great marine biologist or gynecologist too," Mildred answered sarcastically.

"That does it," Barb said and slapped the table. She could feel the eyes of the other diners on her, but she didn't care. "What did your father and I do wrong? You brought me here to ask for my hard-earned money but you are always so disrespectful. I just don't understand. My mother would have knocked the fool out of me if I ever spoke to her the way you speak to me," Barb shrilled.

"Mom, calm down. I was just joking with you," Mildred said seemingly earnest. "Look, I am sorry. I hate asking you for money just as much as I can tell you hate loaning it to me."

"How much do you need?" Barb asked curtly as she tried to regain her composure.

"Just five hundred dollars and fifty-two cents."

"*Just* five hundred dollars and fifty-two cents?" Barb asked.

"Yes."

"That's quite a bit, dear."

Mildred sipped her soda.

"What is the fifty-two cent for?"

"Tax," Mildred offered.

After a pregnant pause, Barb said, "I'll talk with your father, but I can't make you any promises. And I know you don't want to hear this, but you really should think about moving back home. Either that or getting a job."

"You know I can't stand for long periods of time, mom."

"That's why you should take water aerobics with your father and me. You have to do something for yourself. You're young. Imagine how bad off you'll be if you live to be my age. You've got to find purpose and do *something* meaningful with your days."

Mildred finished her final spoon of potatoes and took another bite of toast.

"And what if your father and I should die tomorrow? What would you do then?" Barb asked.

"Don't talk like that, mom."

"Seriously. Your father and I are 87 years old. The good Lord could call us both home tonight. Then what would you do?"

Mildred shifted in her seat and didn't say anything.

"What is your plan, Mildred-Jean?" Barb pressed.

"Do you want to know the truth mom?"

"Yes. I really do."

"Well I *do* have a plan in the event something should happen to you and dad. If my inheritance runs out, I'll participate in medical trials or stuff envelopes for one of those work from home companies or something. They pay pretty good money."

"Are you serious?" Barb asked incredulously.

"Yes. And if that fails, I'll get a couple foster kids."

"Mildee, honey. No case worker in her right mind would entrust foster children to you. You couldn't possibly hide your disdain for kids."

"Mom, just don't worry about me. I'll be alright. If you just give me the $500.52 I hope not to have to ask you for anything else anytime soon."

She didn't want to, but Barb *did* worry about Mildred. How could she not? The world was a cruel place. It was her duty as a mother to protect the gift she'd been given-her precious daughter-her only living child.

Her husband and many others had told her for years that if she continued to bail Mildred out of difficult situations, Mildred would never be able to stand on her own two feet-even as a senior citizen. Barb rejected their predictions, but they were right. Barb hated to admit it, but she had been Mildred's enabler. She had crippled her daughter. And since Mildred's inability to make responsible choices was Barb's fault, Barb would make everything right. It was the least she could do.

Barb looked at her baby girl. She could tell that Mildred meant what she said, but Barb knew that Mildred would need another "loan" within the next 30 days. And quite frankly, she was okay with that.

Barb took a deep breath, smiled at Mildred, and gave her usual response, "You know, I'm sure your father won't mind if I just go ahead and write you the check."

Mildred beamed, "Oh thank you, mom. I *really* appreciate it."

"I love you, sweetheart. I just want you to be happy."

"Oh, I am," Mildred said. "I am."

"And don't mention this to your father," Barb instructed threateningly. She didn't want to hear his mouth.

"I won't," Mildred promised, as she had done countless times before.

They ate the rest of their meal in silence and when the bill came, Barb pulled out her checkbook and paid the balance with a smile.

What did the future hold? Barb didn't know. But at least *she* had purpose. She would continue to provide for her child. Tomorrow she would talk with a financial advisor about ways to maximize the returns on her financial investments. She would do whatever it took to make sure Mildred would never have to participate in research studies, or stuff envelopes, or take in foster children-unless that was what she *really* wanted to do. After all, that's what a good mother would do. Right?

My Love Story

"While the memory of guilt is far from pleasant…it has the curative intent of restoring us into an awareness of the constancy of God's love, new every morning. God's mercy is not spent even with our worst misdeeds."

- Thomas C. Oden
Guilt Free

Readers and listeners sometimes loathe the thought of storytellers flashing back to the beginning. But I'm afraid that if I leave it to others to fill in my blanks, they may add things I never intended to say. They may twist things around to fit their own life's experiences and the story that remains might be something completely different than my own. So please be patient with me as I do more "telling" than "showing" to give you a quick backdrop for my current situation. By the end of my account, I pray it all makes sense. But first, let me introduce myself. My name is Omni, and this is my love story.

Fourteen years ago, I was a freshman in college. I was born and raised in church, but as soon as I was away from home, it was time to put everything I had learned to the test. I was naïve-but I was also curious. And the guy I had been crushing on since Summer Bridge was giving me a little attention. He said I wasn't like any other girls he had met. He told me I was beautiful and he wooed me with his poetry. His voice was so deep. So smooth. When he spoke into my ear and asked if he could show me just how much he loved me I felt a completely new sensation race through my body and I believed that he was "the one."

"Yes," I whispered and let myself go.

The next morning after my Statistics class, I saw him in the hallway. I knew he saw me too, but he walked right past me and put his arm around another girl. He kissed her on her cheek and I could see her melt the same way I had the day before. I was heartbroken. It wasn't even the second month of school and I had already done the one thing I had always said I would not do until I was married.

I was ashamed. The guilt was unbearable because I knew better. I wanted to make things right but I thought it was impossible. I longed for something…anything that would numb my pain and fill the void that my bad decision had illuminated. The voices inside my head didn't have to work too hard to convince me that because I had already gone all the way, there was no reason to stop. My precious title "virgin" was gone and there was no way to get it back.

I had thought I was so perfect, but I wasn't. I was just like everyone else-human. I had believed the lie-that he would like me more and that we would be together forever. And all it took for me to be convinced was a couple months. All it took was a few poorly written poems with made up words to blow my mind and make me forget everything I had been taught.

If I had been in my right mind, I might have thought to re-commit to my initial goal, but I wasn't in my right mind because now I burned. I had tasted the forbidden fruit. Although I knew it was wrong, a part of me wanted more.

I couldn't see clearly. I couldn't think clearly. It was all a blur. Somewhere in my nebulous thoughts, I got the notion that since I had already done things out of order and given myself to a man who didn't love me, I could take back my power by giving myself to as many men as possible without the concept of love in the equation. I might as well experience all the things I read about in magazines and seen in movies. It would take away my heartache, I reasoned.

I changed my goal to something that seemed more attainable now that my innocence was gone. I would become the baddest bad girl. I would master the art of presenting my sweet church girl image in public and my "down for whatever" persona behind closed doors. Men would desire me. They may even want to be more than just "friends," but that would never happen. There would be no love stories. There would be no strings attached. No one would ever hurt me again because I wouldn't allow it.

I compromised so much that I began to feel invincible. I took risks with people whose names and faces now escape me. Soul tie after soul tie after soul tie until one day I looked in the mirror and didn't recognize or like who I had become. But I no longer remembered how to be the "me" I used to be.

By the time I was 21, I was once again hit with the reality of my mortality. My body didn't feel right. I had bumps on my unmentionables and the odor couldn't be ignored. HPV-smaller than the HIV virus (so small it penetrated condoms), could cause cervical cancer, and might prevent childbirth. After the diagnosis I sat in the doctor's office for a while-unable to move-unable to wrap my mind around the fact that I had contracted an incurable disease. I was embarrassed. I felt alone. I didn't have anyone I could talk to.

The new me had caused so much heartache and pain. I wished I could banish her to an uninhabited island. I needed relief, but I didn't know how to get it.

In my distress and in my brokenness I cried out to God from the very depths of my soul. "I'm sorry, God. Please help me. I don't know what to do." And I felt Him ever so clearly invite me to be made whole. He offered to forgive me. He promised to restore me. And in that moment I felt abundant love and sweet peace. I vowed that I would never again give myself to a man who was not my husband.

That was ten years ago. And although I have been tempted many times, I have not broken my promise to Him.

That brings us closer to the present.

A few months ago, my best friend Skylar and I sat on her plush leather couch and sipped fruit smoothies while we looked through pictures from her recent trip to

Chicago. She had spent a weekend there for her family reunion and gave me a brief bio about everyone in the pictures. I could tell from the clothes they wore and the stories she told that they were an interesting bunch.

"Who's that?" I asked, coolly when she got to the picture of a fine specimen of a man who looked to be around our age.

"Girl! Isn't he handsome? That's my fourth cousin, Courtney. He's 35 and lives in Chicago. He's single too, in case you're wondering," she said and smiled.

I was. But first I had to know, "Is he...?"

"Yes. He is saved and sincere."

"How is he your fourth cousin?"

"Girl, I don't know. That stuff is so confusing. I just know he's not my first cousin," she laughed.

I smiled. I could definitely relate. That first cousin once removed stuff was confusing to me too. All I knew was that Courtney was gorgeous. His deep coffee colored skin was very similar to my own. His teeth were big and white, like a chain of Chiclets. And his eyes were inviting. I had never heard his voice but I wanted to hear his life's story and tell him mine.

"He's handsome," I commented, trying not to sound too anxious.

"He thinks you're cute too," she said nonchalantly.

"Wait, you told him about me?"

"You know it," she said and smiled. "And I showed him a million pictures of you."

I could feel my heart beating through my chest.

"I've never heard you mention Courtney before," I said hoping to gauge how well she knew him.

"I haven't talked to him since we were kids," she said, "but I remember that he was super cool back then, and he is just as cool now. I think you should get to know him."

I thought for a moment. He *was* fine. *And* he loved God. Skylar said he was nice. She knew him, but not so well that she would be too involved in our business (should we have any business). This was sounding pretty good.

"Ok. I guess it can't hurt to get to know him. You can give him my number," I said.

"I already gave him your number," she laughed. "But I will text him and tell him to give you a call," she said excitedly as she sent him a message.

I shook my head and laughed. Skylar was my girl. She knew me so well. She was always looking out for me and that's why I loved her.

A few minutes later my phone rang.

It was him.

I answered after the first ring, stepped into Skylar's guest bathroom, and closed the door behind me for a little privacy.

Now I'm going to be completely honest. He didn't sound anything like he looked. His accent was beautiful, but the pitch of his voice sounded like it belonged to a teenage R&B singer. Although that would have ordinarily been a major turn-off for me, for some reason it didn't bother me this time. Courtney had piqued my interest. I wanted to know what he was all about.

We connected on social media and talked every day after that. He told me that he owned a small clothing company in Chicago and I told him that I was an account executive at a boutique marketing company. He was a momma's boy and I was a daddy's girl. He had never been married. Neither had I. He had just gotten out of a long term relationship. I had never been in a serious one. He was raised in a Christian church. So was I.

Courtney did have one strike against him-well two if I counted his voice. He had a daughter. I had always said I didn't want to date a man with children, but I really liked Courtney so I was willing to make an exception-especially since she was 16 years old. He spoke well of her mother and said they hadn't been romantic since their daughter was three years old. They were "co-parenting responsibly," as he called it. I respected that.

Our conversations were usually light and never drifted to the topic of sex. I liked that. Instead, we talked about our favorite books, movies, and entertainers. We told funny stories about our upbringing, talked a lot about our closest friends and co-workers, and usually laughed late into the night-which was 12am Chicago time. Sometimes our conversations were pretty deep. One evening he asked me what I thought about churches who taught that only those who spoke in tongues are saved. Another night he asked my thoughts about life after death and whether I believed in the Trinity. We agreed on the primary issues of faith, but sometimes disagreed about secondary issues. I was ok with that.

I loved that I could talk to him about the things that mattered most to me and he seemed interested, engaged, and genuinely concerned.

About a month ago Courtney told me that he was coming to Los Angeles to spend time with Skylar, meet with a clothing manufacturer in the Downtown District, and meet his future wife in person, if I was available.

Future wife?

My heart raced for a few minutes, but then I remembered that he might not be interested in going that route with me once I revealed my truth to him. Maybe I should save him the trouble of having to wiggle out of talking to me by cutting him loose first.

But I really liked Courtney. I didn't want to end things with him.

I was nervous leading up to our initial meeting. All kinds of superficial thoughts ran through my mind. What if he didn't think I looked anything like my pictures? What if he didn't look anything like his pictures? What if his voice sounded even more high-pitched in person? I hoped that what we had was more special than that. Our biggest issue was surely my situation.

Courtney arrived in town midnight Friday. I met him and Skylar at her condo Saturday morning around 8am. He opened the door after I rang the bell. He was even more handsome in person. His eyes were so very loving. His chiseled body smelled amazing. I was captivated by all that was him.

"Hey, sweetheart," he said. His voice was like a beautiful song as he opened his arms for an embrace.

I closed my eyes, smiled, and leaned in for a hug. I wanted him to hold on to me forever.

I could hear Skylar a few feet away say, "Um…gross. I'm standing right here."

I pulled away from Courtney's embrace and we all laughed.

"It's nice to finally meet you in person," he said.

"It took this moment forever to get here," I said.

"Are you two ready to go?" Skylar asked. "I made a reservation at the place around the corner and Omni, you know how they are."

"Yes. There's always a line and they *will* give our table away if we're late," I said to Courtney.

"Well let's go," he said.

The walk down Laurel Canyon was more peaceful than usual. Fallen leaves and flowers decorated our path nicely. The air smelled of lilac and the sky was bright and full of wispy clouds. Courtney told us that it was extremely cold in Chicago when he boarded the plane but he loved the warmth of a California November. We cut right onto Ventura Boulevard. I could see that the line from The Wa-FULL Joint was already out the door.

"This place is worth the wait," I assured Courtney.

"Yeah. You're gonna love it," Skylar added as we headed to the line for people who had made reservations. There was only one couple ahead of us.

I was thankful Skylar had agreed to tag along with us while Courtney was in town. I hadn't done much dating in the last ten years. I guess I kinda developed a phobia during my wild days about going on solo dates. Those got me into a lot of trouble. I had told her that I was a little nervous and she promised not to leave us alone-unless she got a cue from me.

That's what I loved about Skylar. Some friends would try to make you feel silly for the choices you made-especially when those choices inconvenienced them in any way, but Skylar wasn't like that at all. She always supported me and she was extremely encouraging about my spiritual walk. Our friendship was akin to that of David's and Jonathan's, I imagined. I had her back and she had mine.

Breakfast was excellent, as usual. Courtney said he didn't think Hollywood would have things like chicken and grits on the menu and he was pleasantly surprised because he thoroughly enjoyed it. I was happy he liked our selection.

After walking back to Skylar's we decided to drive to the beach to waste a couple hours before Skylar's boyfriend, Scott, got off work at 4 o'clock. Skylar and I were diehard comic fans, so our plan was to go to the dine-in theatre in Marina Del Rey to see the latest Avengers movie.

On the way to the beach, Skylar and Courtney told so many funny stories about the few times they saw each other growing up. Once, they ran together in a sack race at the reunion BBQ. They were leading the pack, but

Skylar didn't notice the slight hill on her side. She took one wrong step. The two of them found themselves rolling down the hill and they lost the race. They said the worst part was that the family was so competitive that no one even stopped to check on them until everyone had crossed the finish line. The thought of that cracked me up.

The fun continued when Scott joined us. This was his first time meeting Courtney, and they hit it off pretty well. While the two of them chatted about sports and other guy stuff, Skylar and I walked a little ahead and I told her that I was really feeling her cousin.

"I hope that means I will be able to cut some cake soon" she teased.

"You're so silly. I'll buy you a slice of cake that you can cut today," I responded playfully.

"I want to cut *your* wedding cake," she said and we both laughed.

The movie was action-packed. I held Courtney's hand and squeezed it a few times when something unexpected scared me. Each time, Courtney laughed and asked if I was alright. I nodded and blushed. Being with him felt so right.

After the movie we ordered tacos at Baja Fresh and talked for another hour or so about the best tourist spots in L.A. before we headed back to Skylar's and called it a night.

I made it home before midnight, but I called Courtney as soon as I was out of the shower and dressed for bed. We talked until 2am (long after my normal 10 o'clock bedtime) before he encouraged me to try to get *some* rest. Even after we got off the phone I couldn't go to sleep. I felt anxious about our hike.

I really cared for Courtney and I actually believed that he cared for me too. I owed it to him to be honest about my situation sooner than later. It wasn't like I had any intention of sleeping with him before marriage, but I still felt that in the event things did get more serious, my situation would be something he would need to know. Before I went to bed, I thanked the Lord and asked Him to give me the strength to reveal my truth to Courtney.

My dreams that night were haunting. In the first one, I was back at the doctor's office in the exact moment she announced my diagnosis.

HPV. HPV. HPV.

She rattled off a list of symptoms and possible outcomes. My heart ached and I woke up breathing heavily.

When I was finally able to get back to sleep, I dreamt about the many people I had developed soul ties with. I sat in a large room with a rocking chair in the middle and a projector screen on the wall. I was tied to a chair. I couldn't close my eyes. They hurt so badly, but I watched in agony as the faces of my many partners appeared on the screen. "That was fun," each guy would say and then another face would appear and say the same thing. I kept screaming, "No," but I couldn't stop the faces from popping up. I couldn't move. I couldn't close my eyes. I couldn't wake up.

My dreaming image of myself prayed and asked God to help me, and the picture on the screen immediately changed to an episode of "I Love Lucy." Peace and joy washed away my agony and when I awakened, the sun shone brightly through my sheer cotton drapes.

It was 7:45am. I had forgotten to set my alarm. There was no way I could make it to Skylar's house in fifteen minutes. I called and told her that I was running late. We agreed to meet at Fryman Canyon at 9:30am instead. That would give me enough time to do my morning devotional, eat, and shower. Before we hung up I also told her that when we got to the top of the hill, she could leave me alone with Courtney so that I could talk with him for a few minutes.

I took a deep breath.

I poured myself a cup of orange juice and sat on the couch in my living room for a few minutes of fellowship with God. Nothing was more important than my quality time with Him. I thanked the Lord for His forgiveness and asked Him to help me forgive myself again. I hated that even though so many years had passed, sometimes I still found myself feeling guilty. I thanked Him for Courtney and asked that whatever today's outcome, we would at least remain friends.

When I arrived at the beginning of the trail, Skylar and Courtney were already there, stretched and ready. Skylar's boyfriend had to work so it was just the three of us.

"Sorry I'm so late," I said to Courtney.

"That's because you were up talking all night," Skylar teased knowingly.

"Aw. Leave her alone, Sky. She was talking to her man," Courtney said beaming.

I blushed.

"Her man? Ok, ok. I can already taste the cake," Skylar said and winked at me.

I blushed and shook my head. She was so silly.

Courtney gave me another one of his comforting hugs and a peck on the cheek.

"I like your hair like that," he said.

"Thank you," I said sweetly as I fluffed my 'fro and soaked in his aura.

The walk started out a little difficult for Courtney. It was obvious he hadn't been hiking in a while. Skylar and I walked a lot slower than usual so that he wouldn't be too embarrassed by his inability to keep up.

Courtney said that he really enjoyed the views. "L.A. is my kinda place. I could see myself living here," he said, and looked at me out the corner of his eye.

I smiled. That *would* be nice.

Skylar said, "Yeah. My first year here was crazy, but you couldn't pay me to move back to Tennessee."

"I think most of the transplants I meet feel the same way. They move here, hate the people, start to actually get to know the people, decide they love it here, and then denounce their hometowns," I said laughing.

"That is so true," Skylar agreed.

As we neared the mulch and bench that marked the start of the downward descent of the hike, Skylar said that she was going to jog the rest of the way and would meet us in the parking lot afterward.

I told her that we were going to stop and rest for a few minutes before continuing on.

"If you want, maybe we can just meet you at The Wa-FULL Joint in about an hour," Courtney suggested.

"Sounds good. I'll make the reservation when I get back to my car," Skylar said and jogged off.

Courtney and I made our way to the benches and sat down. He obviously appreciated the break.

We sat in silence for a couple minutes before he finally said, "I'm out of shape."

"No!" I said sarcastically and giggled.

He nudged my arm and that made me laugh even more.

"I see how it is," he said. "You guys do this all the time."

"Yeah. It was your first time. It gets easier when you get used to it," I said to make him feel better. He held my hand and a chill ran through my body.

"There's something I want to talk to you about," he said.

I shifted a little. "What's up?"

"Well, these past couple days have been the best two days of my life. I don't want you to think I'm crazy or anything like that because I know we've only been talking for a few months, but I love you Omni."

My heart stopped beating for a few minutes. No guy had ever said that to me. His words were like honey.

I blushed, "You know-I love you too."

He squeezed my hand and I could see excitement in his eyes.

"I'm not one to play games and I don't like to waste time. There's no doubt in my mind that you're the one.

I knew it when Skylar first told me about you. I just got this feeling. And then when she showed me your picture I was blown away. You're beautiful-inside and out," he said.

I was flattered. I felt the same way about him. The only thing was that I had a secret that might affect his feelings for me. I pulled my hand away from his and said, "Look, there's something I need to tell you."

He grabbed my hand again. "What is it?"

"Well, I know you know that I am celibate."

"I completely respect that," he said.

"Well, I wasn't always celibate. I was pretty wild during my college years."

"I don't care about your past," he assured me.

"The thing is I picked up an unwanted package in my past that remains with me in my present and will follow me into my future, if you know what I mean."

"I already know about that, and I don't care," he said.

I held my breath. "What do you mean you already know?"

"Skylar mentioned the unwanted package the first day she told me about you-even before she showed me your picture. I don't care, Omni."

I was confused. Were we talking about the same thing? Why would Skylar tell him something so personal and not mention it to me? That didn't sound like something she would do. But then again, if she had indeed told him, she'd done me a favor. Although if she had told me that she told him I wouldn't have wasted so much energy worrying about his response.

"What exactly did she tell you?" I asked.

"Don't be mad at her. I told Sky I wanted to know *everything* about you-and not just the good stuff. She told me that you are one of the most amazing women she has ever known, that you are compassionate, that you are encouraging, and that you truly love the Lord. She said that the only thing she could think of that might be a turn off was the unwanted package from your college days. She told me that it led you to a lifestyle change and that you have been true to your promise to God ever since."

"Wow," I said as I tried to process everything.

"I have so much respect for you, Omni. So many people make promises to God, but very few are actually able to follow through with them. I admire that you actually kept your promise. I know how difficult it must be at times."

"So we *are* talking about HPV, right?" I whispered just to be sure he really did know.

"Yes," he said and laughed. "And I have done my research on it. I'm not afraid, and it doesn't make me love you any less."

I exhaled. Finally.

I felt an ocean of love and acceptance flood my being. It made me think back to that day in the doctor's office. I had felt so ashamed. So hopeless. So filthy. But God had been right there with me offering something that the world hadn't been able to give me. He wanted me to be so full of Him that there wouldn't be room for anything else. I remember feeling more strongly than ever that I was forgiven and loved. That kind of love from my Father-the kind that would love me in spite of all that I had done in rebellion and disobedience-made me want to live a different lifestyle. It made it easy to shake off the habits that had only led to hurt and disappointment. God's true love meant more than anything to me. And now God had blessed me with Courtney-a good man who truly loved Him and me.

Before I knew it, tears streamed down my face.

"Don't cry, sweetheart," Courtney said and kissed me softly on my cheek.

"I'm just so happy," I said.

He held me in his arms as we overlooked the captivating canyon below.

"Now we just have to figure out whether you're moving to Chi-town or if I'm moving to L.A. because I'm gonna marry you."

I liked the sound of that.

I wondered what it was like in Chicago. That's one place I had never had any desire to visit. But honestly, I didn't mind moving to Antarctica as long as I could be there with Courtney. He was truly an unexpected gift from God…and I looked forward to spending a lifetime with him.

That was yesterday. Today, Courtney and I have plans to eat breakfast together at The Coffee Company before I drive him to the airport for his 12 o'clock flight.

I don't know the details of the future, but I trust God to write our love story. He's the Master Author. He always weaves things together beautifully – unexpectedly – perfectly - just as they are meant to be. And in the end, all glory is due to Him.

The Collector

"First you're young, then you're middle-aged, then you're wonderful."

-Alice Longworth Roosevelt

The wall-to-wall mirror hung snugly above the 1950's pink tile that adorned the bathroom sink. Matilda gave herself one final look. Her chocolate chip face framed lines of wisdom that formed beneath her hazel eyes. Thin salt and pepper hair, which she always parted on the right side and neatly bobby pinned in the back, lay more perfectly than usual. Matilda put on her Gilligan hat, gently rubbed a dab of Oil of Olay on her entire face, and headed out to the car, where her husband, Walt, sat patiently waiting.

Sunday evenings were her favorites. "Treasure Evenings," she called them. As the sun set, she and Walt would put on the matching sweat suits their oldest son, Junior, got them for their 35th wedding anniversary.

Each week, rain or shine, they cruised around Baldwin Hills and View Park in their '94 Galant hunting for the goodies people left out for Monday morning's trash pick-up. Each week Matilda found multiple trinkets to clean up and display in her own cluttered living room.

Walt complained about their home being overly crowded but was always ready to leave for "Treasure Evenings" before Matilda was, which proved he enjoyed dumpster diving as much as she did.

After Matilda strapped herself in, Walt started the car and pulled off slowly.

"You look nice, Mattie," he complimented as he glanced at her admiringly.

"That's because I've got that feeling," she said loudly.

"Well, that's a good sign," he smiled as they reached the first stop sign on Don Felipe Drive. Palmettos and broadleaf trees, beautiful even in the fall, were sprinkled between the stacked homes lining the street.

Matilda knew her fire was what initially attracted Walt to her. Although she wasn't into antiques or collectibles when they met 40 years ago, she *was* obsessed with finding and saving the pennies people dropped. At the time, her plan was to save $250 in coins and donate it all to the NAACP.

The day she met Walt, she was on her lunch break walking down Pico Boulevard, with eyes glued to the ground. Lost in her thoughts, she tripped over her foot and ended up on the sidewalk, knees and hands scraped. That's when a tall, mature chocolate brownie of a man with wavy black hair and a mustache that put Fredrick Douglass's to shame rushed to her side.

"Are you ok?" His voice was a bass guitar.

"Yes," Matilda said, embarrassed. She could feel her cheeks flush.

Walt extended a hand to help her up. "My name is Walter Williams. It's a pleasure to meet you."

"Matilda Coffins," she returned, entranced by the rhythmic way he said his name.

For the rest of her lunch break, they sat at the Corner Deli on Pico and La Cienega chatting about her $250 objective. Walt told her many times after that first meeting that the thought of her finding and saving $250 in coins for charity is what made him fall in love with her. Her actual completion of the project, according to Walt, is how he knew that she was the one. He asked her to marry him shortly after she reached her goal.

Forty years and three children later, they were still together. Many things had changed, but one thing stayed the same-Walt loved her, quirks and all.

Matilda was careful not to talk too much. His hereditary hearing impairment along with years of work with loud machinery at Uniroyal Tire Company had all but murdered Walt's hearing. Mattie had to turn her volume up a couple notches whenever she conversed with him. If she didn't he would either smile and nod and pretend to hear her or, if he was interested in her topic of choice, he would say a little too loudly, "REPEAT." The "REPEAT" startled Matilda every single time he said it. She hated that, so she tried to say things as loudly as she could to avoid it. Even more than the loud "REPEAT," she hated the dull shrill his hearing aids made whenever they weren't adjusted properly. Walt couldn't hear them, but Matilda was sure people as far away as South Africa could.

He would lean in with his eyes still on the road to hear her better. The speedometer would drop from 30 to 20 and sometimes even to 15. The drivers behind them would swerve to get around him or vehemently honk their horns to get him to go faster. She didn't need any of that today-at least not *before* they made it to Angeles Vista Street.

Walt adjusted the dial to KFWB, news 980, and resumed driving, looking straight ahead. His eyes weren't as good as they used to be. Matilda, who was 16 years his junior, was the "lookout woman." At 72, she had eagle's eyes and could spot goodies from miles away.

Walt made a right turn off Stocker Street and onto Valley Ridge Avenue. Matilda's eyes lit up. The street was lined with treasure. She spotted an old television set at a modest home a few houses from the corner on the left side of the street. She smiled picturing her grandchildren watching it during their holiday visit.

"Honey, stop the car!"

Walt pulled to the side of the road and Matilda hopped out. She rushed across the street to examine the 13" set. The antenna was missing and the cord was ragged. It also lacked a volume control knob along with the buttons that indicated channels.

Perfect.

After a little fixing up, the television would be as good as new. She wondered how this generation had become so wasteful. When she was a child, nothing salvageable was ever tossed. You might pass on clothes to younger siblings, but you NEVER just threw good things away.

Matilda braced herself, lifted the television, and gently placed it in the trunk, which Walt had routinely popped from inside the car. She smiled and returned to the passenger's seat.

"You know that old thing isn't any good, sweetie," Walt said matter-of-factly. "There's no way I can get it working and looking good."

Matilda stared at Walt with cat eyes, cold enough to pierce holes through steel. One thing she absolutely loathed about Walt was his belief that if he couldn't fix something it couldn't be fixed. He was certified as a carpenter, technician, and mechanic many years ago, but times had changed. In fact, most of the gadgets he fixed around the house over the past five years blew up and had to be thrown away almost as soon as he fixed them.

Matilda looked ominously at Walt. Her eyes darkened. "I didn't ask your pot to boil, honey."

Walt looked at her for a moment, jaws clenched, and then turned back to the road. He put the car in drive and

Matilda pleasantly instructed him to drive up two houses.

Her next destination was the statuesque two-story brick home with a "For Sale" sign on the lawn. The fire-engine red door reminded Matilda of the red overcoat that her daughter wore when she was a young girl. She remembered how adorable her daughter looked on Christmas morning in 1976 with her red velvet colored afro puffs, white ruffled dress, red overcoat, and dimpled peanut butter brown skin. Everyone always complimented Matilda on how well she coordinated her daughter's look.

The sidewalk in front of the brick house displayed all kinds of exciting goodies. From her experience as a collector, Matilda knew that the best treasures were in the trash of those who were moving. They threw away perfectly good things because they didn't fit in with the color schemes in their new homes. Matilda would find a way to make them fit in with her white walls and dirt brown carpet.

She rummaged through the pile that decorated the curb and found items that were true beauties-an oil painting of orange and yellow flowers with long green stems on a swirling blue background, three oddly shaped glass vases, a couple romance novels, a bust of Abraham Lincoln, a flowerpot, and an antique-looking cherry wood coffee table. She couldn't wait to get home and clean them. She beckoned for Walt to come and help her carry her jackpot to the car.

***

The next morning, Matilda woke up early and prepared for her daily 7am walk. She walked outside and stretched on the pavement in front of her garage while she waited for Belle. It was a gorgeous day. White cumulus clouds were sprinkled across the endless blue sky. She looked down the hill and could see the skyscrapers of downtown L.A.-beautifully nestled against more modest buildings.

The homes in her Baldwin Hills were amazing. After the fire in the late '80s, many of the residents had rebuilt mansions, each outdoing the next. Matilda and Walt's home was one of the few that remained standing after the fire. It was minute compared to the others but it was Matilda's palace. She loved it just as it was. Matilda closed her eyes and breathed the crisp air. She thanked God for allowing her to enjoy all the beauty around her.

At 7:15am Belle sauntered up to Matilda. She wore a black Bebe Sport sweat suit, a black baseball cap, and large gold dangling earrings. Belle didn't leave the house without her full face and jewelry on. She was 20 years Matilda's junior, nouveau riche, and fabulous. She was a Southern Belle, who had met her husband, Harry while they both vacationed in Bermuda. They fell in love-she with his money and he with her beauty-and moved to Baldwin Hills after their extravagant marriage in the Bahamas.

Matilda made it a point to meet everyone who lived within five homes of her on either side of the street, so when Belle moved in, she was the first neighbor to greet her with a homemade pound cake and a smile. They were both domestic engineers, which meant they were able to bond during the day while Matilda's children were at school. They borrowed eggs from each other and called each other to talk about Oprah or The Young and the Restless from time to time.

Although Matilda was old enough to be Belle's mother, their friendship didn't resemble the mother-daughter relationship. They were more like dear friends who lived 3,000 miles from each other and were close because of their differences rather than their similarities.

Belle was flashy. Matilda was modest. Belle dyed her grays. Matilda embraced hers. Belle liked modern things. Matilda absolutely loved antiques. Belle had a model's figure. Matilda could stand to lose a pound or two-or three. Belle loved to talk about everything under the sun. Matilda's topics of interest could be counted on one hand. And yet, slight drizzle or shine, these two managed to get together every morning to walk, and the walks were never boring.

"Hey, Tilly. Sorry I'm late. Harry wanted me to fix breakfast before he went to work today," Belle said in her signature southern drawl. She had lived in Los Angeles for years, but hadn't been able to get rid of the accent.

"No problem, chil.' It gave me a chance to stretch," Matilda said as she jogged slowly in place.

Belle always had the inside scoop on the neighborhood happenings, and Matilda listened intently as she filled her in on the latest gossip.

About halfway through the walk, Matilda decided to share the details of her previous evening's voyage.

"Oooh, Tilly. You have to show me the things you got."

"Not today. I can't let you in my junky house," Matilda said playfully as she picked up a shiny nickel and smiled. Money still had a way of finding her.

"You know I don't care about a little junk. Every week you tell me about the good things you find, but you won't show me."

"My house has more than a *little* junk," Matilda said with a chuckle. She glanced at Belle, who looked disappointed, and felt a twinge of remorse. "I'll tell you what. If I can get things somewhat organized by Friday I will let you have a peak. Deal?"

"I'm looking forward to it," Belle said smiling.

Matilda stopped to pick up a nail and place it in someone's bushes.

They walked on, discussing the neighbors' marriage problems, financial woes, and anything else Belle chose to mention.

An hour later they finished their conversation in front of Matilda's house.

"I'll call you at 11," Belle promised. "This is the episode where Victor is killed and raised from the dead. It's gonna be juicy, honey."

Matilda laughed and bid her farewell.

Inside, Matilda put on a pot of Yuban coffee and sat down at the kitchen table. It was littered with newspaper clippings, coupons, sales papers, bills, letters, and sheets of scrap paper that held her grocery lists. She cleared a space on the table in front of her seat and cut out the "Love is…" section, which she planned to mail to her youngest son. After finishing the morning "Jumble" and reading a portion of "Dear Abby," the coffee was ready. She poured a cup and called her daughter in Missouri. Matilda knew that she had already left for work, but wanted to leave her a message to let her know that she was on her mind.

"Hello, my dear child. This is mom. I just called to say hi and let you know that I love you." She blew kisses into the phone and gently hung up as she heard Walt's footsteps approach.

"I smell coffee," Walt said loudly as he slowly entered the kitchen.

"Good morning, honey," she returned sweetly.

Walt walked to Matilda and greeted her the way he had for 40 years. "Hol' ya jaw…" He gave her a peck on the forehead. "Taw, taw!"

Matilda could tell that Walt was in a great mood.

The phone rang and Matilda answered it. It was for Walt. She handed it to him, finished her cup of coffee, and headed out to the back patio. Two small lizards were in their usual position-on the concrete next to Matilda's flowers. They appeared to do push-ups when they saw her and she smiled.

"Good morning, Suzie and Samuel," she spoke to them. They stopped moving long enough for her to imagine them saying good morning back and then they scurried off toward the collard greens growing around the side of the house.

Matilda doubted anyone had a more breathtaking view of the city than she and Walt did. The sun, which wasn't visible from where she stood, made its presence known by illuminating the beauty below. Mount Baldy and downtown were backdrop to sweet gum trees, palm trees, and palmettos that dotted the peripheral hillside and homes.

"Good morning, roses! Good morning, tomatoes!"

Matilda smiled and leaned in to kiss the petal of one of her white roses. She took a deep breath and removed her outdoor scissors from their home on a shelf near the sliding glass door. She cut one white rose and one pink rose each three inches long and took them into the house where she could enjoy them. She placed them, along with an aspirin, into a medium blue vase and set them on the kitchen table. They took the edge off the clutter.

Walt was in a deep conversation with one of their tenants about the plumbing problems they continued to have. Matilda could never figure out why Walt didn't just call a rooter service, or even hire an apartment manager to handle rental issues. He was 88 years old, yet he refused to give himself a break.

Matilda fixed herself a breakfast of oatmeal, bacon, eggs, toast, and another cup of coffee. She no longer fixed Walt breakfast because of his self-proclaimed bad stomach. According to him, he was allergic to anything she cooked. When he got off the phone, she was sure he would fry himself some salt pork, poach an egg, and make toast.

She sat down at the table and finished reading "Dear Abby." She skimmed through "Ann Landers" while she ate breakfast and made plans for the rest of her day.

The first thing on her list was to dust the organ that sat awkwardly between the sliding glass door and the buffet in the kitchen. Walt hadn't played the organ a day in his life and although it was grossly out of place, he refused to get rid of it, insisting that it had sentimental value for him. Sometimes Matilda pictured it in front of their own home on trash day, but Walt made it clear that most of the things in their home belonged to her and he would be very hurt if she threw away his one item.

After Matilda dusted the organ, she attacked the cluttered buffet. Those two tasks alone took two hours to complete.

***

On Thursday morning, Matilda finally got around to cleaning up some of her findings from the previous weekend. She stood in the hallway and looked around the living room. *What a mess.* There was a decaying wood table, a matching buffet, and a record player in the middle of the room. She could smell them from where she stood. She already had someone in mind to give the buffet to and planned to have the table and record player refurbished for her own enjoyment. On top of these three items were her daughter's old Cabbage Patch dolls, pots, books, dishes and other things that she planned to clean and then display in the front bedroom, which was *officially* dedicated to her collectibles. Next to the big screened television that she'd found on a hunt a few years back were two stereo cases filled with trinkets she hoped to have appraised someday.

There were two dated rocking chairs that she'd had re-upholstered, and a faded coral colored couch that she found on one of her Sunday missions. An out of tune upright mahogany Baldwin sat in the corner, and pictures of her three children hung on the walls above it. A treadmill was positioned along the wall opposite the piano. There was a porcupine looking piece of iron that held up her glass top table. On it were a collection of Ebony and *O* magazines that she kept neatly organized for guests, should any ever stop by. She didn't anticipate the latter and couldn't even say that she would let a guest in if they should knock, but she was prepared nonetheless. There were also fresh roses and odd vases on the glass top table.

Matilda pulled open the drapes to let in a little light. Seeing the windows reminded her that they hadn't been cleaned in ages. She made a note to hire a cleaning lady for that since she didn't do windows.

The television she found on Sunday evening was already in the repair shop. The gentleman who agreed to fix it said it would be ready within a week. She made a mental note that she needed to clear a place for it in the guest bedroom before it came back.

Matilda picked up the Lysol spray and silver polish and gave her goodies the attention they needed to reach their fullest potential. She worked for four hours and then decided to take a nap. She would invite Belle in for a look the next day.

***

"You have so many beautiful things, Tilly," Belle complimented.

"Thanks, girl! I'm starting to get some things ready to give away."

"Really?" Belle asked.

"I'm telling you, I raised three children in this home. Now that they're gone, the house has gotten smaller. I'm going to have to let go of some things."

Matilda watched Belle's eyes as they made their way to the patio.

"My God!" Belle gasped.

"I had to set some things out there until I can find a space for them in here. I know they're worth a small fortune. I tell Walt all the time that people throw away valuables, not realizing what they're worth."

"That is so true! I wish I had the time and patience to collect," Belle said, her eyes dancing around Matilda's treasures.

"It really doesn't take much time for the trained eye. Maybe you can go with me to the thrift shop one day next week. They have great bargains at the ones in Santa Monica."

"Maybe."

"Have a seat. I'll get you some tea."

"No thanks," Belle said nervously.

"Why not? I was hoping you could stay a little longer."

"I have to get going. Harry likes his dinner on the table when he gets home."

"Aren't you a good wife?" Matilda teased. "Okay. Well take this with you," she said and handed Belle a clear flower vase with a bright red rose inside.

"Tilly, this is beautiful," Belle said as she took a whiff of the rose. Her eyes began to tear up. "Thank you so much!"

"Oh Belle, no problem at all."

Matilda smiled and walked Belle to the door.

***

The next Monday after Matilda's morning nap, she noticed a letter from the Baldwin Hills Homeowners' Association in her mailbox. She took it into the kitchen and sat down before opening it.

July 15, 2015

Homeowner's Association

Dear Mr. and Mrs. Walter Williams,

Quite a few neighbors have complained about the junk on your patio. It is visible from the bottom of the hill. Please remove the rubbish from your patio and yard within the next thirty days or we will notify the Department of Health Services of your non-compliance. A fine will be assessed.

We appreciate your prompt attention to the matter.

Signed,

Harry Johnson

Matilda wondered whether Belle had been the cause of the letter. She hadn't been so angry since the time Walt bought another rental property on Mace Place without consulting with her first.

Matilda called Belle immediately.

"Belle!"

"Oh hi, Tilly. How…"

"I received a letter today signed by your husband," Matilda interrupted. "Do you know anything about it?"

Belle hesitated. Matilda could hear her searching for the right words. Matilda wanted to strangle her. She had been kind enough to let her in her home, and Belle had been plotting against her the whole time. She should have known better than to trust Belle and her oceanic mouth. Matilda had even given her one of her most beautiful vases only to be betrayed.

"Tilly, it's not what you think. A lot of neighbors have been complaining. They say your house is bringing down property values."

"Well why didn't you tell me, Belle? We walk every morning. You tell me what's going on with everyone else."

"Tilly, I'm sorry!"

"So when you came over here the other day, was it really to see my antiques or had you been sent by the association to report on the 'junk' in my house…You know what? Don't even answer that question. Just tell your husband I got the letter."

"Tilly, I'm so sorry," she heard Belle say as she hung up the phone. There was no reason to say goodbye.

Sorry is right.

That night Matilda lay next to Walt in their king-sized bed. It was the only thing in their cluttered room, aside from their clothes and shoes they had actually bought. Matilda's lamp was on and Walt watched the ten o'clock news. A familiar silence enveloped them. Matilda stared blankly at the ceiling.

"Are you going to tell me what's got you upset?" Walt asked still looking at the television.

"Honey, I received a letter from the Baldwin Hills Home Owners' Association today stating that we have to clear off the patio. Supposedly there have been some complaints and they are threatening to report us the Department of Health Services. People *obviously* don't understand that it takes time to cultivate sand into a pearl," she said on the verge of losing her cool.

Walt frowned. His brownie-colored skin had become more wrinkled than she ever imagined it would 40 years ago. His eyes looked sunken in and the wrinkles in his large forehead were intensified by shadows cast by the television.

Then, more calmly, "You think we could borrow Sylvester's truck and take a load of things down to the storage on San Pedro."

"My goodness, Mattie. This is just terrible. I will call 'Vest in the morning. I bet you those Turners are the ones who complained. I speak to them every morning, and they look at me and move their mouths, but I know they aren't saying hi back," Walt replied. He frowned a little more and Matilda knew that he was just as upset as she was.

Matilda thought about it for a second. The Turners lived 3 doors up the hill in an extravagant two-story home. They always sat on their front porch and stared at her when she returned from the Council Thrift Shop on Tuesdays. Come to think of it, they did seem to reluctantly return her hellos. Walt might be on to something.

"Let me start from the beginning," Matilda started. "Last week Belle asked me to see my treasures. I didn't think anything of it because I didn't have a reason to."

She continued on and explained the whole story exactly as she saw it. Walt leaned in to listen intently while she spoke, nodding and asking questions from time to time.

She felt comfortable talking with him. It was just like it had been years ago when the kids were home. They talked about the cleaning situation for at least an hour. They determined that the storage on San Pedro probably wouldn't hold all the things on the patio, so they would rent a unit at the facility on Rodeo and La Brea. They also made plans to eventually clean out the garage so that Matilda could park her car in it. Walt suggested they call their oldest son to see if he could fly out to orchestrate the cleaning venture. Matilda agreed that that was an excellent idea.

After figuring out the patio situation, they found themselves reminiscing about the great times that marked their existence together. Walt told her for the first time that on the day they met, he had laughed so hard when he got home and replayed the fall in his head. He told her that the fall was so graceful and she looked so miserable and that he was so glad that he had been there to help her up that day.

"I love you so much, Mattie."

"I love you too, Walt."

They laughed and laughed like they hadn't in a long time. Walt held Matilda in his thin arms for the first time in years and kissed her gently on her forehead. He turned on a midnight recap of the Antique Road Show. Silence returned, but this time it was different. It was peaceful. Matilda was happy. She was no longer angry at Belle. In fact, she would call her in the morning to apologize for hanging up in her face. Her thoughts began to jumble and as she drifted, she smiled to think that soon the television would be watching them.

www.ingramcontent.com/pod-product-compliance
Lightning Source LLC
Chambersburg PA
CBHW060153180626
46813CB00007B/2733